BC503596

East
Mountain
Man

DATE DUE

FEB 1 3 2007	JUL 3 1 2016
FEB 0 9 2008	MAR 0 4 2017
MAR 0 1 2008	OCT 1 0 2017
MAY 0 5 2008	DEC 0 5 2018
MAY 1 7 2008	
APR 2 2 2009	
APR 1 2 2010	
OCT 0 1 2010	
DEC 1 6 2011	
APR 0 2 2012	
MAY 0 8 2012	
JUL 0 9 2012	
JUL 2 1 2012	
JUN 0 3 2013	
AUG 1 9 2013	
NOV 2 9 2013	
FEB 2 6 2014	
SEP 1 1 2015	

GAYLORD   PRINTED IN U.S.A.

BL

DESTINY OF THE MOUNTAIN MAN

Also by William W. Johnstone in Large Print:

Ambush of the Mountain Man
Code Name: Coldfire
Code Name: Death
Code Name: Quickstrike
Cunning of the Mountain Man
The First Mountain Man: Preacher's Justice
The First Mountain Man: Preacher's Peace
The Last Gunfigher: Manhunt
The Last Gunfighter: No Man's Land
The Last Gunfighter: The Burning
The Last Gunfighter: Violent Sunday
Power of the Mountain Man
Quest of the Mountain Man
Warpath of the Mountain Man
Wrath of the Mountain Man

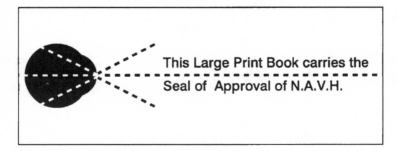
This Large Print Book carries the
Seal of Approval of N.A.V.H.

WILLIAM W. JOHNSTONE WITH FRED AUSTIN

DESTINY OF THE MOUNTAIN MAN

Thorndike Press • Waterville, Maine

Published in 2006 by arrangement with Pinnacle Books, an imprint of Kensington Publishing Corp.

Thorndike Press® Large Print Western.

The tree indicium is a trademark of Thorndike Press.

The text of this Large Print edition is unabridged. Other aspects of the book may vary from the original edition.

Set in 16 pt. Plantin by Christina S. Huff.

Printed in the United States on permanent paper.

Library of Congress Cataloging-in-Publication Data

Johnstone, William W.
    Destiny of the mountain man / by William W. Johnstone with Fred Austin.
        p. cm. — (Thorndike Press large print westerns)
    ISBN 0-7862-8543-5 (lg. print : hc : alk. paper)
    1. Jensen, Smoke (Fictitious character) — Fiction.
2. Texas — Fiction.   3. Large type books.   I. Austin, Fred.
II. Title.   III. Thorndike Press large print Western series.
PS3560.O415D47 2006
    813'.54—dc22   2006002272

DESTINY OF THE MOUNTAIN MAN

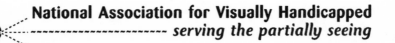

As the Founder/CEO of NAVH, the only national health agency solely devoted to those who, although not totally blind, have an eye disease which could lead to serious visual impairment, I am pleased to recognize Thorndike Press* as one of the leading publishers in the large print field.

Founded in 1954 in San Francisco to prepare large print textbooks for partially seeing children, NAVH became the pioneer and standard setting agency in the preparation of large type.

Today, those publishers who meet our standards carry the prestigious "Seal of Approval" indicating high quality large print. We are delighted that Thorndike Press is one of the publishers whose titles meet these standards. We are also pleased to recognize the significant contribution Thorndike Press is making in this important and growing field.

Lorraine H. Marchi, L.H.D.
Founder/CEO
NAVH

* Thorndike Press encompasses the following imprints: Thorndike, Wheeler, Walker and Large Print Press.

Prologue

1870:

The Golden Nugget Saloon in Pueblo, Colorado Territory, was already a beehive of activity, even though the Regulator clock sitting against the back wall indicated that it was just after twelve o'clock in the afternoon. A man with a two-day growth of beard and red-rimmed eyes was plinking away on a piano in the corner of the room while a glass of warm beer, its head gone, sat beside him. Two cowboys stood at the bar, engaged in a vociferous discussion as to the relative merits of rye versus bourbon. One of them punctuated his argument by expectorating a large quid of tobacco into a nearby spittoon, making it ring with the impact. A soiled dove, whose profession had already caused dissipation beyond her years, adjusted her low-cut evening gown as she made the rounds of the tables, letting the customers know, by flirtatious smiles and intimate touches, that she was available

7

for business. She was trying to sing in tune with the piano, but was failing miserably.

All sound and activity stopped, however, when two men slapped the batwings open, stepped into the saloon, and crossed over to the bar. Everyone in the place paused and stared at the pair as they made their way across the room. They looked like perfect examples of what life in the mountains would do to anyone crazy enough, or antisocial enough, to endure it.

The older of the two had fought in the Battle of New Orleans as a fourteen-year-old boy. The younger of the two was a boy during the Civil War, which had been over but five years. Despite their age differences, there was a strong similarity between them. Both were dressed in buckskins that were almost black with accumulated trail dust and dirt and grime, and both had full beards and long, unkempt hair that hung down almost to their shoulders. The older man's hair was white, while the younger man's hair was the color of dark smoke. It was obvious from their appearance and smell that they'd been up in the high country for some time, without benefit of a bath.

They belonged to that most reclusive of breeds — mountain men — but it wasn't the fact that they were mountain men that caused everyone in the Golden Nugget Saloon to stop what they were doing and stare. Mountain men weren't all that rare in this part of Colorado Territory, especially in winter when storms would sometimes drift the snow deep enough to drive even those hardy souls down to civilization. What caught everyone's attention was the fact that they were armed to the teeth. The old man was carrying what looked to be a Sharps Big Fifty cradled in his arms, and a Navy Colt .37 stuck down in his belt. The younger one had enough weapons to start a war: A Navy Colt was tied low on his thigh in a right-hand rig. A matching Colt was butt-forward in a high holster on his left hip, and a twelve-inch-long bowie knife rested in a scabbard in the middle of his back. A Henry repeating rifle was slung across his shoulders to complete the picture.

The young man's eyes were as hard and uncompromising as new ice on a pond, while the older man's expression was one of whimsy, as if he'd seen just about all that was worth seeing in his many years and saw little now that would impress him.

When the older man set his rifle down and they both leaned on the bar, all but one of the saloon customers went back to what they'd been doing, ignoring the two odd-looking newcomers. One of the customers, however, Bradford Preston, continued to stare at the two.

Though it was still early in the day, Preston had already had more than enough to drink. If you asked, Preston would call himself a cowboy, though he found work only sporadically, due to his temper, hardheadedness, and the fact that not many cattlemen trusted him. It had never been proven, but there were those who suspected that Preston would sometimes support himself by cutting out a few head of cattle, butchering them, then selling the meat and the hide.

Preston drained his glass and slammed it down on the table, nodding his head at one of the others sitting with him to refill it from the almost empty bottle on the table. "Damn, Johnny," Preston said in a loud, grating voice, "it smells like a skunk done up and died in here! Why don't somebody open up some windows or something to get the stink of those two mountain hombres outta my nose?" he called out to no one in particular.

The younger man's back stiffened and he started to turn around, until the older man put a hand on his arm.

"Take 'er easy, Smoke," he said in a low

voice. "It's just a young pup with too much whiskey in his gullet tryin' to impress his friends. If'n you try 'n shut all of them kind'a beavers up, you'll wind up takin' on a job you ain't never goin' to be able to finish."

Smoke Jensen nodded and took a deep breath as he looked at Preacher and grinned. "Now I know why we spend so much time up in the high lonesome away from assholes like that."

Smoke hadn't bothered to keep his voice low and Preston heard his remark. He jumped to his feet, wobbled for a second, and then walked over to stand just behind Smoke. "Hey, you stinkin' pile of shit, did you just call me an asshole?"

Preacher sighed. "Now the fat's in the fire."

Smoke turned to face Preston. The belligerent drunk was standing less than three feet away from him, and Smoke stared at him with a face totally devoid of expression.

"Yeah," Smoke said easily. Moving his right hand slowly, he unfastened the rawhide hammer thong on his right-hand Colt. "I did."

Preston blinked a couple of times. He had expected Smoke to deny it, or talk around it, or at least show some anxiety over being called down on it. He did not expect the young man to show such dead, cool calm.

"Them's fightin' words, mister," Preston said angrily, his fists balling at his sides.

Suddenly, and inexplicably, Smoke laughed. "You're too drunk. If you want to fight, get a wife," he said. "My partner and I just want to have a couple of beers in peace and be on our way." Smoke started to turn back around, but Preston's voice stopped him.

"That ain't gonna happen now," Preston said angrily. "I'm callin' you . . ." he began, and slapped at his pistol.

Before he could clear leather, Smoke's pistol was in his hand and, taking a step forward, he laid the barrel of his Colt across the drunken man's cheekbone, slashing it open and knocking him to his knees. Preston wobbled once, and then his eyes crossed and he flopped to land face-forward on the wooden floor. Blood began to pool around his face and soak into the planks.

Smoke spun his pistol once and replaced it in his holster, glaring at the men at Preston's table who'd gotten half out of their chairs and were staring at him.

"Anyone else here object to my friend and me having a quiet drink?"

Johnny Dean, one of the other men who

had been at the table with Preston, whispered in a hoarse voice full of awe, "Good God Almighty, boys, I didn't even see him draw!"

Smoke reached down, pulled Preston to his feet, and looked at the bleeding wound on his face. "You boys might want to take your friend over to see a doctor. That cut's gonna need some stitches."

"Yes, sir," one of the men said as they grabbed hold of a still-stunned Preston.

Johnny Dean hesitated. "Uh, did I hear your friend call you Smoke?"

"That's what they call me."

"Smoke Jensen?" Dean asked, his voice quaking a bit.

"Look, friend, I'd like to carry on a conversation with you, but right now I have a beer that's getting warm on the bar."

When he turned to the bar and picked up his glass, Preacher whispered, "Better hurry up and drink it, Smoke. I don't figure we've got too long 'fore somebody informs the sheriff that we're here."

Smoke nodded. He still had a price on his head up in Utah from when he'd taken on the gang of outlaws, and he never knew just where those pesky wanted posters were going to turn up. Preacher was right; it was better to drink up and be on their way before trouble found them again. And, he had noticed, trouble did have a way of finding them if they tried to stay planted for too long in one place.

It seemed, Smoke thought, you could outrun a man or a posse, but you could never outrun your reputation.

Smoke had just put his empty beer glass down on the bar when a group of several men crowded through the saloon batwings and gathered in the doorway. The man at the head of the pack was a couple of inches over six feet tall and had wide shoulders, a beer gut that hung over his belt, and a Greener ten-gauge shotgun cradled in his arms.

Johnny Dean came in with the sheriff, but he made a point to be standing behind him. From that position, he pointed toward Smoke and Preacher. "There they are, Sheriff, jest like I tole you! Them's the two men what pistol-whipped poor ole Preston and damn near tore his cheek plumb off'n his face."

Smoke stared at his accuser and, trembling, Johnny took a few steps back.

Smoke looked at Preacher and shrugged. "Sorry, Preacher. Looks like we might've waited too long."

Preacher smacked his lips as he let his

hand drop to the barrel of his Sharps. "Yeah, I think you are right. But I do believe the beer was worth it."

The man Dean had called "Sheriff" raised his shotgun to point at them. "I'm Sheriff Tom Jackson, boys, an' I'd be obliged if you'd drop them irons on the floor. We don't take kindly around here to strangers comin' into our town and assaulting our citizens."

Without speaking or looking at each other, Smoke and Preacher eased apart until they were separated by a few yards.

"Sorry, Sheriff," Smoke said in a low, dangerous voice, his eyes as hard as emeralds and his face set in stone. "But we won't be droppin' our guns."

Jackson's face expressed surprise and he cut his eyes down at his Greener. "Are you boys blind? You do see what I'm holdin', don't you?"

Smoke smiled and peered at the shotgun. "Looks like a W.W. Greener ten-gauge double-barrel shotgun to me. What do you think, Preacher?"

"I'd say you're right. You might remember that ole Dooley had him a Greener just like that."

"Yeah, I do remember. Whatever happened to Dooley anyway?"

"Don't you recall? He married up with that Indian woman he had took to livin' with. I think they went up into Dakota Territory somewhere."

"Oh, yeah, that's right."

The sheriff followed the conversation, turning from one to the other as they spoke. The expression on his face went from curiosity to incredulity.

"What the hell? Are you two men daft? You're carrying on a conversation like you're taking a walk around town. You do see that I've got this gun pointed at your guts, don't you?" the sheriff asked.

"Which one of us?" Smoke asked.

"What?"

Preacher grunted. "What my friend is tryin' to tell you, Sheriff, is that you haven't cut the barrel down none."

Jackson raised his eyebrows. "What's that supposed to mean?"

Smoke grinned, though there was no mirth in his smile. "What it means, Sheriff Jackson, is that if you pull the trigger on that thing, you're going to die, same as if you was to put the end of the barrel in your mouth."

"What? My God, are you totally crazy?" Sheriff Jackson asked.

"Maybe I should explain," Smoke continued. "Because you haven't cut the barrel down, your scattergun's gonna throw a pretty tight pattern at this distance. That means you can only get one of us if you pull the trigger."

Preacher nodded, but his lips were tight and thin and in a straight line, no evidence of a smile on them. "And that means, pilgrim, that 'fore the echoes of your shot are done bouncin' off'n these walls, you'll be lying dead on the floor, no matter which one of us you shoot." He glanced around the room as he pulled back the hammer on his own pistol. "And in all likelihood, a whole bunch of yore townsfolk are gonna git kilt in the process too."

Johnny Dean started easing away from the sheriff and the possible line of fire.

"Won't do you any good to move, friend," Smoke said. "You'll be the next one killed, right after the sheriff."

"What? Why me?" Dean asked.

"Because you're the one who brought the sheriff over here," Preacher said.

The sheriff's eyes narrowed. "I don't believe either of you two are that fast," he said, but his voice was suddenly hoarse and beads of sweat appeared on his forehead.

"Uh, Sheriff," Dean said, "I kind'a forgot to mention that man's name there on the left is Smoke Jensen, and I do believe I heard him call the other gent 'Preacher.' "

Jackson's Adam's apple bobbed and you could hear him swallow clear across the saloon, which was now deathly quiet.

"You men are Smoke Jensen and Preacher?" he asked, his voice dry and husky with fear. Just about everyone west of the Mississippi had heard of Jensen and Preacher, and the sheriff knew that no one had ever gone up against them and lived to talk about it.

Smoke nodded, while Preacher just leaned his head to the side and spit a glob of tobacco juice into the brass spittoon several feet away. It hit dead center.

"Well, uh," Jackson stuttered, trying to think of some way out of his predicament with his hide intact. "What you got to say for yourself 'bout slappin' a pistol in Preston's face?"

"You know Preston, do you, Sheriff?" Preacher asked.

"I know him."

"What kind of a man is he?"

"What do you mean?"

"I mean, if you know him, do you really think my friend here just slapped him for the fun of it? Or do you think maybe Preston might have brought it on himself?"

The sheriff cleared his throat. "I reckon he's the kind that might have brought it on hisself."

"He tried to draw on me," Smoke said. "And it was either slap some sense into him or shoot him dead. Would you rather I'd killed him?"

Before the sheriff could answer, a thin young man in a suit and vest stood up from a corner table. "Sheriff Jackson, if I may. I witnessed the entire episode and I can vouch for the veracity of these gentlemen's account."

"Huh?" Jackson said, his forehead wrinkling.

"What I'm saying is, they are telling you the truth." The young man smiled and walked up to the sheriff and handed him a card. "My name is Robert Justus Kleberg and I am chief counsel for the governor of the Colorado Territory."

Jackson heaved a sigh of relief and for the first time let the barrel of his Greener drop. "Oh, well, if the lawyer for the governor says he's tellin' the truth . . ."

"But Sheriff," Dean called from halfway across the room. His beady eyes were narrow and angry. "Jensen's got a price on his head. Everybody knows that! You've got to arrest him and put his ass in jail where it belongs."

"You want me to take a chance on getting my ass killed just so you can collect some reward?" Sheriff Jackson asked.

"Well . . . that's your job . . . ain't it?" Dean asked.

Kleberg leaned close to the sheriff, whispered a few words in his ear, and the sheriff nodded, relief evident on his face. "Mr. Kleberg here says he's gonna take Mr. Jensen and his friend over to the hotel to meet with the governor and that'll be the end of it."

"But . . . !" Dean cried.

Sheriff Jackson glared at Johnny Dean. "My advice to you, Johnny, is to shut up 'fore I run you in for disturbin' the peace. You and that drunk Preston are the ones started all this in the first place. Now let's get the hell outta here and let Mr. Kleberg do his job."

Once the sheriff, Dean, and Preston's other friends were gone, Kleberg walked up to Smoke and handed him one of his cards. "Mr. Jensen, Preacher, if you don't mind coming with me over to the hotel, I'd like you to meet the governor."

"They got a bar in that there hotel?" Preacher asked. "I still got me some trail dust needs washing outta my throat."

Kleberg smiled. "I am sure libations can be arranged."

"What?" Preacher asked.

"He said yes," Smoke said as they followed Kleberg out of the saloon.

"Say, Mr. Kleberg," Smoke said as they walked down the street toward the hotel, "any particular reason you want us to talk to the governor?"

Kleberg smiled. "First, please call me Bob. When I hear someone say mister, I always look around to see who they are talking to."

Smoke glanced at Preacher and grinned. He was beginning to like this young man. He wasn't full of himself like so many of the lawyers Smoke had met in the past. "Sure, Bob, but that didn't answer my question."

Kleberg looked over his shoulder at Smoke. "I know," he said. He smiled, but didn't add anything else. "This way," he added, holding his arm out.

Kleberg showed them through the large doors that led into the Palace Hotel; then they went straight across the lobby toward a room off to the side. "Since it's lunchtime, I suspect he'll be here in the dining room," Kleberg said.

"Dinin' room?" Preacher protested. "I ain't hungry, I'm thirsty!"

As they walked past a man wearing a suit jacket and a horrified expression on his face,

Kleberg snapped, "Pierre, bring my friends here anything they want to eat or drink. We'll be at the governor's table."

"But Mr. Kleberg . . . their conduct, their mode of dress . . ." the head waiter protested.

Suddenly Smoke saw the steel in Kleberg's makeup. He turned cold eyes on the waiter and snapped, "Are you questioning the attire of guests of the governor, Pierre?"

"Wh . . . uh . . . no, sir!" the waiter answered, all but clicking his heels together before he turned to Preacher and Smoke with a wide, but obviously forced, smile on his lips. "What would you gentlemen like to drink?"

"A couple of beers would be nice," Smoke said.

"And I'll have the same," Preacher drawled, pulling the lapels of his buckskin coat together as if that could somehow make up for the several pounds of dirt embedded in his clothes.

The waiter looked at them as if he hadn't quite understood the order.

"Bring them two beers, Pierre," Kleberg said. He paused for a moment, then with a smile, added, "Each. Didn't you hear what they said?"

"Very good, sir," the waiter replied.

Moments later they were standing before a large round table, at which sat a rotund man in a three-piece suit of black wool. He wore his hair rather long and had a large, ornate mustache that drooped down almost to his chin.

At first glance, he was a typical politician, Smoke thought, self-important and arrogant. However, when the man raised his eyes, he didn't gasp at their soiled appearance or ask Kleberg what he meant by bringing such disreputable-appearing men before him. Instead he smiled, got to his feet, and held out his hand.

"Good afternoon, gentlemen," he said. "I'm Governor William Gilpin, but please call me Bill."

Smoke took his hand. "Hello, Governor. I'm Smoke Jensen and they call this old reprobate next to me Preacher."

Preacher sniffed and grumbled, "I ain't old. You're just a wet-behind-the-ears pup is all."

Gilpin raised his eyebrows. "You're *the* Smoke Jensen?"

Smoke nodded. "Only one I know of."

"Forgive me for staring, Mr. Jensen, but I didn't realize you were so young."

"He's young, but he's been rode hard and

put up wet, Governor," Preacher drawled, "an' he's got an awful lot of miles on him."

Gilpin smiled and motioned to the chairs around the table. "So I hear, Preacher, so I hear. Please, have a seat, gentlemen. Did Bob tell you we'd been talking about you the last couple of days?"

Smoke frowned. "No, he didn't."

At Smoke's look, Gilpin held up his hands. "Oh, no offense, Mr. Jensen. We were just remarking that there are some men in the territory who have . . . um . . . shall we say, have had more than their share of life's experiences."

He paused while the waiter brought in a tray with four beers.

"Kleberg, you know I never drink beer," Gilpin said.

Kleberg chuckled. "All four beers are for these two gentlemen," he said.

Gilpin joined in the laughter. "Then by all means enjoy them, gentlemen. Would you care for some lunch?" he asked.

Preacher pursed his lips for a moment, and then he nodded. "I could use me a beef-steak, just charred enough to keep it from movin', some fried taters, an' maybe some canned peaches if you have 'em."

Smoke grinned. "Preacher dearly loves canned peaches. I'll have the same."

The waiter looked at Gilpin.

"Bring them what they want," Gilpin said.

"You were saying something about our . . . life's experiences?" Smoke asked. He set the words apart.

"Yes," Gilpin continued. "You see, gentlemen, Congress and President Grant are going to make Colorado Territory a state any time now, and it is my feeling that men like yourselves, men who've helped tame this country and make it safe for us Easterners, are going to be sorely needed in the next few years."

"You hirin' outlaws, Governor?" Preacher asked before draining his first glass of beer.

"No, no, you misunderstand me. Bob has gathered a stack of warrants and wanted posters on most of the wanted men in Colorado, and we've investigated the charges against them and found most of them valid. We aren't interested in those men." He leaned back and took a long, black cigar out of his coat pocket. He took a moment to light it, and not until he was puffing easily, and his head was wreathed with smoke, did he continue. "But from what we can tell, Mr. Jensen, every time you've been charged with murder, you've been acting in self-defense."

Smoke snorted. "Well, now, Governor, I wouldn't exactly go that far. It's true that I've never killed a man that wasn't tryin' to kill me at the time, but I gotta admit that some of those times I kind'a forced their hands a mite."

Kleberg nodded. "We know, Smoke, and we've found out that every one of those times, the men you killed had wronged you first by killing someone in your family."

"He's right there, son," Preacher said. "Ain't neither one of us ever kilt nobody that didn't deserve it — an' deserve it in spades."

"So, we all agree, we're a couple of saints," Smoke said, laughing. "But just what do you have in mind, Governor?"

Gilpin leaned back and shifted the cigar from one side of his mouth to the other. He smiled. "You tell them, Bob. It was your idea."

Kleberg looked from one to the other. "The governor is going to issue you both full pardons for all crimes you've been charged with up to now. You'll both start with a clean slate as far as the law is concerned."

Smoke's smile was replaced by a look of shock. This was a tremendous offer. He couldn't remember the last time he'd ridden into a town and not had to look over his shoulder to make sure the law wasn't gunning for him.

"We're certainly grateful for that, Governor, but just what do you expect from us in return?"

"Nothing, son, absolutely nothing," Gilpin said around his cigar. "Just go on doing what you've been doing. The stories of your exploits and the exploits of men like you will do more to bring civilization to this territory than all the government bureaucrats in Washington can."

"You see, Smoke, when ordinary men back East read about your adventures, they will want to come West to live like that themselves," Kleberg said.

Smoke chuckled. "Well, Bob, let me tell you. It reads a whole hell of a lot better'n it lives."

Just then Pierre showed up with two trays containing their steaks. He grimaced at the blood oozing from the barely cooked meat as he placed the plates on the table.

"Just a minute," Preacher said, picking up his fork. "Let me stick it to make sure it's dead enough to eat."

Chapter One

Ten Years Later:

Nearly 2500 cows stood quietly in the pre-dawn darkness, gathered during the spring roundup. The cows gathered represented but a tiny percentage of the over 100,000 head that occupied the rangeland of the 825,000-acre Santa Gertrudis Ranch. When 7500 more head were gathered, Richard King, the owner of the ranch, would start the long, long trail drive up to Dodge City, Kansas, where the cattle would be put on trains for markets in the East.

From the small breakfast fire the cook had kindled, glowing orange sparks rode a column of hot air to join the stars in the pre-dawn darkness. One of the cowboys at the camp reached for a coffeepot, but jerked his hand back quickly when he touched the handle.

Ted Abbot laughed. "Hot, is it, Carter?"

"Not all that hot," Roy Carter replied.

Carter took his hat off and, using it as protection, picked up the coffeepot a second time.

"Anybody else want any?" he asked after he poured himself a cup.

"*Gracias*, Carter, I'll take a cup," Ramon Gonzales said. Though he was a Mexican in the midst of a bunch of Texans, Ramon was the top hand, appointed to the position by Richard King, the owner of the ranch, and readily acknowledged as such by the other cowboys.

"And I too shall imbibe of your fair brew," one of the cowboys said, holding out his cup.

"Harbin, you are as full of shit as a Christmas goose," Carter said, chuckling.

"Say us a poem, Harbin," one of the other cowboys said.

Harbin stood up and folded his right hand across his heart while he held his left out before him, striking an exaggerated orator's pose.

> *"She walks in beauty, like the night*
> *Of cloudless climes and starry skies;*
> *And all that's best of dark and bright*
> *Meet in her aspect and her eyes."*

"Hey, speaking of night, who's ridin' nighthawk?" Emil Barrett asked.

"Noble, Tanner, and Gillis," Ramon said.

29

"It's about time they come in, isn't it?"

"Hell, they're prob'ly on the other side of the herd, sound asleep," Carter suggested, and again, the cowboys laughed.

"Ramon, you've made cattle drives before," Abbot said. "How long does it take?"

"Two months," Ramon answered.

"Two months? That's not so bad," Harbin replied.

Carter chuckled. "Not so bad for you. You're going back East to go to school, so you won't be making the drive."

"I've never made a drive," Abbot said. "What's it like?"

"It's like nothin' you've ever done," Carter said. "You'll be working seventeen-hour days, seven days a week, on very little grub, with no tents, no tarps, and damn few slickers. The horses will get tired and their backs will get so sore that they'll fight you when you ride them. And the worst thing is no sleep. Five hours when the weather is nice, maybe an hour when it isn't. But that don't matter 'cause you'll have to do another fifteen miles the next day whether you got 'ny sleep the night before or not. Sometimes you'll find yourself rubbing tobacco juice in your eyes, just to keep awake."

"Oh, damn, that hurts just to think about it," Abbot said. He pretended to rub tobacco juice into his eyes, then squinting, squatted down and flailed about. The others laughed at his antics.

On the other side of the herd, nearly sixty men rode through the dark of a copse of scrub oak trees. Shadows within shadows, they moved quietly to the edge of the trees, then fanned out into one long flanking line.

The leader of the group was wearing a Union officer's jacket of the style worn some fifteen years earlier during the Civil War. The shoulder epaulets had major's bars on a yellow field, indicating cavalry.

Jack Brandt, who was no longer in the Army but still insisted upon being called Major, stood in his stirrups to stretch out just a bit, then settled back into the saddle.

"Look at all them cows," one of the men near him said. "What do you say, Major, that we cut out a hundred head or so, then run 'em across the border and sell 'em down in Mexico?"

"No," Brandt said.

"But to just ride down there and kill 'em seems like such a waste."

Brandt glared at the man. "Preston, you knew what you were signing up for when you enlisted."

Although Brandt was no longer in the

Army, he ran his outfit as if it were an Army unit. Because of that, suggesting that the man had "enlisted" came natural to him.

"You heard the major's plans," Sarge said. Like Brandt, the man, whose real name was Stone, but who preferred to be called Sarge, was wearing a blue Army tunic. On his sleeves were the stripes of the rank he'd once held. "All we have to do is fix it so's nobody will work for him and he'll go broke, plain and simple. Then we'll have our revenge."

"Yeah, well, revenge is good," Preston said. "But it don't buy you no whiskey or women."

"Think about it, Preston. In a few weeks, he's going to be drivin' ten thousand head or so all the way to Kansas," one of the other men said. "If he don't have nobody to work them cows, they'll be as easy to gather up as apples that's fallen from a tree. You are talking about stealing a hundred head. Hell, we'll be able to take ten thousand head with no problem."

"Yeah," Preston said. "Yeah, I guess I can see that."

Brandt, who had not joined the conversation, pulled his sword.

"It's not dawn yet so, like as not, the night riders are still out there. We'll take them first."

Of the three nighthawks, Noble, who was nineteen, was the oldest. At sixteen, Tanner was the youngest, and he came in for a lot of teasing from the other two.

Tanner had dismounted and was relieving himself.

"Damn, listen to that boy pee, will you?" Noble said. "He sounds like a cow pissin' on a flat rock off'n a fifty-foot cliff."

Gillis laughed. "Hell, when peein's the onliest thing you use your pecker for, you bound to be able to pee hard. Wait till he has him a woman. She'll take some of that steam out of him 'n he won't be able to pee so hard."

"How do you know I ain't never had me no woman?" Tanner asked as he buttoned his pants.

" 'Cause iff'n you'd'a had yourself a woman, you wouldn't be able to shut up about it. That's all we'd be hearin'," Gillis said.

From the darkness, a calf started bawling.

"Damn, some little feller's wandered off from his mama," Noble said. "Guess I better go get'im back."

"It's time to go in now, ain't it?" Tanner asked. "I know they got breakfast ready and I'm hungry."

"You was born hungry," Noble said. "We'll go in soon as I get back." He clucked at his horse and rode toward the sound of the bawling calf, disappearing into the darkness.

"I ain't, you know," Tanner said.

"You ain't what?" Gillis asked.

"Had me no woman."

Gillis chuckled. "Hell, there's got to be a first time for everything. Just wait until —"

Gillis's comment was interrupted by a loud, bloodcurdling scream.

"What? What the hell was that?" Tanner asked.

"I don't know. It sounded like Noble. Noble? Noble, you all right?" Gillis shouted.

"Gillis, I'm scared," Tanner said.

Gillis pulled his pistol and when he did, Tanner pulled his as well.

"Noble? Noble, are you out there?"

"Wait a minute," Tanner said suddenly. "Are you two trying to run a shuck on me?" He chuckled. "That's what you're doin', isn't it? Trying to scare me?"

"Tanner, I swear to God, I don't know what this is about," Gillis said.

They heard the sound of a horse coming at a trot. Then the horse appeared from the darkness.

"That's Noble's horse, but where is he?"

Gillis asked. Clucking at his own horse, he rode toward it, then suddenly stopped. "Oh, my God!" he shouted, turning away. "Oh, my God!"

"What is it?" Tanner asked. Then he saw what Gillis had seen. There, mounted on the saddle horn, was the disembodied head of Ned Noble.

"Harbin, I think you, Jenkins, and Kelly should ride out to relieve Noble and the others," Ramon said back at the cow camp. "They should've been in by now."

"Your wish is my command," Harbin replied. Nodding at the other two men Ramon had selected, he said, "Come, my noble fellows, we few, we happy few, we band of brothers."

"Harbin, where do you come up with all that shit?"

"That's from Shakespeare's *Henry the Fifth*," Harbin said as the three started toward the remuda. They had just cut out their mounts when a very large group of men burst out of the trees, firing.

Harbin went down with the opening fusillade.

"What the hell!" Barrett shouted.

The men swept through, firing as they galloped through the camp. One of them had a rope, and as he passed the chuck wagon, he threw a rope around a high stake, then pulled the wagon over. The cowboys were totally surprised by the attack, and many of them weren't even wearing guns. The few who were armed began firing back.

The attackers made two more passes through the camp, then rode out into the herd, shooting at the cattle as they rode by. The cattle began dropping.

"My God, they're killing the cattle!" Carter shouted.

"Who the hell are these people?" Barrett asked. "Where did they come from?"

"I don't know, but there sure as hell are a lot of them. Ramon, we need to get mounted! We need to get after them!" Carter said. "Ramon?"

Looking over at Ramon, Carter saw the top hand leaning back against the over-turned wagon. Ramon's right arm was hanging down by his side, his pistol dangling from a crooked finger. His left hand was covering a wound on his right shoulder, and blood was spilling through his fingers.

By now, the sound of gunfire was receding as the attackers had passed through the herd and rode off on the far side of the valley. The cattle, spooked by all the shooting, were milling around, but had not stampeded.

"I think they are gone," Barrett said.

"Emil," Ramon said to Barrett, his tight voice evidence of the pain of his wound. "Ride back to the big house, tell Mr. King what just happened."

"All right," Barrett replied. He nodded toward the wound. "But you better get yourself into town and get that bullet hole looked at."

"I'll see that he does," Carter said to Barrett. "You better get started."

Richard King had never done anything on a small scale. When he was eleven years old, he became dissatisfied with his apprenticeship in New York and stowed away on a schooner. Discovered, he had to work for his passage. After a few years learning the shipping trade from the bottom up, including becoming a captain, King took a partner and formed his own shipping company. By the late 1840's, his company was shipping supplies for General Zachary Taylor along the Rio Grande.

Enamored with Texas, Captain King settled there, started ranching, and by 1860 he and his new bride, Henrietta, had grown their various enterprises into an 860,000-acre ranch along the banks of the Santa Gertrudis River in Texas.

Ever the businessman, King invested in building railroads, icehouses, packing-houses, and harbor improvements in Corpus Christi, Texas, which was just forty miles from his ranch.

Now, the ranch owner was planning the logistics of a cattle drive to Dodge City, Kansas. He had considered shipping them to Kansas by rail, but the circuitous railroad route it would require to make all the connections would take two weeks, and it would cost him approximately four dollars per head, or forty thousand dollars. Driving the herd to Dodge would take eight weeks, but it would only cost him about three thousand dollars total.

King was sitting at his desk, working out the logistics of the drive, when Emil Barrett came in to see him. Standing in front of the big oak desk, holding his hat in his hands and nervously rolling it by the rim, he made his report to his boss. Barrett's jeans and shirt were covered with dirt and dust and he smelled of sweat and cows, but Captain Richard King took no notice of that. He did wonder why the young cowboy was here, instead of out on the range, helping with the roundup.

"What are you doing here, Barrett?"

"Cap'n, we got trouble," Barrett said,

addressing him as Captain, as did all the cowboys.

"What sort of trouble?"

Barrett told of the predawn attack.

"How about you, Barrett, are you all right?" he asked.

"Yes, sir, I'm fine. I would'a still been out there with the others iff'n Ramon hadn't'a sent me back to bring you the news."

"Ramon was right, and you did well. Go to the kitchen, get yourself some coffee and whatever you want to eat."

"Thank you, sir," Barrett said.

After Barrett left, King stood up from behind the enormous oak desk in his study. He was an imposing figure of a man. Almost six feet tall, he had broad shoulders and heavily muscled forearms that made the paunch he was developing in his later years seem smaller. His hair was streaked with gray and was beginning to thin out a bit on top, but his mustache was thick and black and still full.

He walked over to a clothes tree in the corner where there hung a right-handed holster rig. Taking it down, he buckled it around his waist with the familiar motion of someone who had worn a gun before. He pulled the Colt Peacemaker from the holster and spun the cylinder to make certain that every chamber was loaded. Satisfied, he put the gun back into its sheath, then took a large Stetson hat from the rack, placed it on his head, and adjusted the brim before walking out of his study and into a slightly smaller office next door.

Robert Justus Kleberg looked up from his desk and frowned when he saw the old man wearing his sidearm. "Going hunting, Boss?" he asked. Kleberg was young, in his mid-thirties, and rail-thin, without an ounce of fat on his six-foot-one-inch frame. His face was pleasant without being classically handsome, and his hair, the color of caramel candy, was slightly rumpled in front as if he'd been out in a strong wind.

"Get your pistol and follow me, Bob. Seems that we have a problem," the old man ordered gruffly.

Kleberg looked slightly startled. King had hired him a couple of years earlier to handle the legal tasks for his Santa Gertrudis Ranch, and as such his duties didn't normally entail wearing a pistol. Not that it mattered much. Kleberg had grown up in the nearby town of Corpus Christi, which was a haven at the time for Mexican *bandidos* and Civil War deserters, so he'd been proficient with a six-gun from the time he was old enough to carry one.

40

Kleberg took his holster and pistol rig off a peg in the wall and blew the dust off before he buckled it around his hips. He started to put his suit coat on, but decided against it since it looked as if he and the old man were going for a ride. No need to get the coat dusty and dirty.

As they walked through the enormous rooms of the ranch house, Alice King, Richard's daughter, stepped out of the kitchen with a pan dulce pastry in one hand and a cup of steaming coffee in the other.

When her eyes met Kleberg's, her cheeks flushed crimson and she stopped in her tracks. Her eyes traveled down, and she noticed both her father and the man she'd fallen in love with were wearing pistols.

"Where are you two going?" she asked, glancing down at her hands. "I was just bringing Bob a pan dulce and a cup of coffee."

In spite of his sour mood, King grinned. He loved his daughter with every fiber of his being, and to make matters even better, he approved of her choice of Bob Kleberg as the man in her life. He knew Kleberg to be smart, ambitious, fearless, and he also knew that Kleberg loved his daughter as much as he did, which was just icing on the cake.

Kleberg stepped quickly to her side and

41

took the sweet roll from her hand. "Thank you, Alice," he said. "Your father is going to show me something and I'll eat it on the way."

"But Bob," she asked, a worried look on her face, "why are you wearing a gun?"

King moved up next to her and put a hand on her shoulder. "There's been some rustlers seen out on the range, dear. We're just being cautious. Nothing for you to worry about." He leaned down and pecked her on the cheek. "We'll be back before you have time to miss us."

"Before I have time to miss you?" Her eyes cut to Kleberg and her lips turned up in an impish smile. "That won't take very long, Papa."

Now it was Kleberg's turn to blush.

King laughed and put a hand behind Kleberg's back and shoved him toward the door. "Come on, Bobby, we're burnin' daylight."

Chapter Two

King and Kleberg rode for almost an hour until they finally came to the banks of the Santa Gertrudis River. The river, for which the ranch had been named, was running swiftly over rocks and sandbars and while as deep as eight feet in some places, here it was only about three feet deep. They urged their horses out into the water, rode across quickly, then climbed up onto the bank on the other side.

From there they could see the cow camp where the cows to be driven north were being gathered. Several men were standing around the wagon. One of the wheels was broken on the wagon, and the side was stoved in. It was obvious, even to the most casual observer, that the wagon had been turned over and set back upright. As they got closer, they saw at least thirty cows, maybe more, lying sprawled in the pasture. Closer still, and they saw a row of bodies lined up neatly on blankets. Five were un-covered, three were covered by tarpaulins.

"Damn," King said as Carter came out to meet him. "Damn, how many?"

"We had eight killed," Carter answered, nodding toward the bodies.

"Oh, shit," King said, looking at the bodies. "Stan Harbin is one of them."

"Yes, sir," Carter said.

King pinched the bridge of his nose. "I just got a nice letter from his mother. He was going back East to go to college."

"Yes, sir, he was tellin' us all about it," Carter said. "Goin' around here quotin' poetry and all that."

King saw two other bodies lying to one side. They had been drawn together, but they weren't lying on a blanket, or even a tarp.

"Those two part of the rustlers?" King asked, pointing to the two dead men.

"Yes, sir, sort of," Carter replied.

"Sort of? What do you mean, sort of?"

"Well, sir, they were part of the group that attacked us, but they wasn't exactly rustlers," Carter said. "Leastwise, not so's you could call them as such."

"Well, if they weren't rustlers, what were they?"

Carter shook his head. "I don't know as I can rightly answer that question," he said. "They just come in here and commenced shootin'. Wasn't interested in stealin' nothin' as far as I could tell. All they was interested in was killin' as many of us as they could. They shot the hell out of us, along with all the beeves they could hit." He shook his head. "It wasn't nothin' more'n a slaughter, I mean, what with us not suspectin' anything 'n all. Most of us wasn't even wearin' guns at the time."

"That wasn't very smart, was it?" King asked. "Not wearing your guns, I mean?"

"Cap'n King, it was just breakin' dawn. We'd just rolled out of our blankets. And why would we need our guns then? I mean, who would'a thought . . ."

King waved him down before he finished. "I'm sorry," King said. "Of course you wouldn't be armed. And why should you be? I shouldn't have said anything."

"Well, here's the thing, Cap'n. Two of them fellers was wearin' Army uniforms."

"Army uniforms? Wait a minute, are you telling me the Army did this?"

"No, sir, I don't think so. I mean, they was only two of 'em wearin' anything like that, and they was just wearin' the jackets of a uniform is all."

"I'll be damned. That's strange," King said. He looked around. "I don't see Ramon. Where is he? Is he all right?"

Carter shrugged. "Far as I know, he is. He took a bullet in the shoulder, never said nothin' about it till he'd already seen to all the others. I talked him into lettin' one of the boys take him into Benevadis in a buckboard so's the doc could take a look at it. He still didn't want to leave, but I told 'im there wasn't nothin' more he could do out here."

"You did right to send him into town. How many would you say there were in the group that did this?"

Carter snorted. "A hell of a lot of 'em," he said. "That's all I can tell you. There was just a hell of a lot of 'em."

"What? Five, ten, twenty?"

"More'n twenty," Carter said. "More'n fifty I would say."

"Fifty?" King replied, surprised by the number. "Are you telling me that fifty men did this?"

"At least fifty, maybe more."

King shook his head and turned away to look out over the carnage. "Bob, what the hell are we facing here?" he asked quietly. "Who would get fifty men together to steal a few cows?"

"Especially since they didn't steal any," Kleberg observed.

That was when King saw that three of the

bodies were covered. He turned back to Carter.

"Who are the three men under the tarps?" Kleberg asked, pointing toward the three covered cowboys.

"That's Noble, Gillis, and Tanner," Carter said. "Only thing is, we ain't real sure which one is which."

"What do you mean?"

"They ain't got no heads," Carter said.

"What?" Kleberg gasped.

"They ain't got no heads," Carter said again. "Their heads was cut off."

"Their heads were cut off?"

"Yes, sir."

King was quiet for a long moment, and he stroked his chin as he considered the situation. "I wonder if . . ." he started, then he stopped. "No, it can't be," he said.

"What can't be?" Kleberg asked.

King shook his head. "Nothing," he said. "It probably isn't the same thing at all. I'm sure I'm just imagining things."

"What are we going to do about all these fellas that was killed?" Carter asked.

"Send someone in town to get the undertaker," King said. "And bring them back to the ranch. We are going to give them a decent burial. And find their heads," he added, pointing to the three tarp-covered bodies.

"Yes, sir. We need to do something about the cows that was killed too."

"Take the hides, get what meat you think we can use, then get them in a pile and burn them," King ordered.

"And . . . what about them two galoots?"

King looked over toward the two bodies of the raiders, then hawked up a spit.

"Burn them with the cows," he said coldly.

Big Rock, Colorado:

Smoke Jensen was in Longmont's, enjoying a beer, when someone stepped inside.

"Is Smoke Jensen in here?" he called out.

"I'm over here, Howard," Smoke said, holding up the mug of beer he was drinking. He was sharing a table with his friends, Sheriff Carson and Louis Longmont, the owner of Longmont's Saloon and Restaurant.

"Maybe you better step outside, Smoke," Howard said. "There's a couple of fellas out there givin' Miss Sally a hard time."

"Are they town people?" Sheriff Carson asked, standing at the table.

"No, Sheriff, I ain't never seen either one of 'em before."

"I didn't think anyone from town would do anything like that," Carson said.

Still carrying his beer, Smoke walked over to the front door and stood there, looking over the top of the batwings out into the street. He took a swallow of his beer.

"Ain't you goin' to go out there and help her?" Howard asked.

"Nah," Smoke said. He chuckled. "There's only two of them. Let Sally fight her own fights."

"What do you think, Speeg? You think you can show this little lady a good time?"

The speaker was a young man, around twenty, tall and gangly, with large teeth and a scraggly beard.

"That ain't the question, Hoke," Speeg answered. "The question is, is she going to show *us* a good time?" Hoke was standing at the hitching rail, holding onto the team that had pulled Sally's buckboard into town. Speeg was alongside the buckboard, and both of them were smiling up at Sally Jensen, who was sitting in the buckboard seat.

"Let go of my team," Sally said.

"Nah," Hoke said, his leering grin growing larger. "I don't want to do that. If I do that, you might run off a'fore we have a chance to get to know each other."

"Yeah," Speeg said. "If you'd get to know us a little better, why, you'd like us."

"I doubt that even your mothers like you," Sally said.

Speeg laughed. "Whooeee, she's a feisty little thing, ain't she, Hoke?"

"I like 'em feisty," Hoke said. He grabbed himself in the crotch. "What do you say, little lady? Let's me'n you'n Speeg there get us a bottle and go off an' have us a good time some'eres."

"I don't suppose it matters to you that I'm married," Sally said.

Speeg shook his head. "Nope. It don't matter to us none a'tall."

"You see, we ain't exactly wantin' to marry you," Hoke said. "We just want to borrow you for a bit."

"Yeah," Speeg said, laughing at the concept. "That's what we want. We want to borrow you for a bit."

Sally took the whip from its holder. "I'm warning you," she said. "Go away and leave me alone."

"Ha! And if we don't?" Speeg said, starting toward her.

Moving more quickly than Speeg could react, Sally jammed the butt of the whip into

Speeg's nose, breaking it. He let out a yell and took several steps back, putting his hand to his nose to stop the bleeding.

"What the hell?" Hoke shouted, but that was as far as he got before the whip slashed across his face, instantly blackening both eyes.

"Why, you bitch!" Speeg shouted in anger. He started toward her, but stopped when Sally shot his hat off.

Sally sensed Hoke coming toward her, but she didn't turn to face him. Instead, she aimed her pistol at Speeg's groin.

"Unless you want to squat to pee for the rest of your life, you'll call your friend off," Sally said, calmly.

"Hoke, no, wait! Wait! Hold it!" Speeg shouted anxiously, holding out his hand.

"You two men are strangers to our little town, aren't you?" Sally asked.

"Yes . . ."

"Ma'am," Sally said.

"What?"

"When you speak to me, it's yes, ma'am."

Speeg glared at her, and Sally pulled the hammer back on her pistol. The sound of her cocking the gun was quite audible.

"Yes, ma'am," Speeg said.

"I thought so. And that being the case, I think everyone would be happy to see the two of you climb up onto your horses and leave."

"You ain't the sheriff. You don't have no right to run us out of town," Hoke said defiantly.

Sally smiled, a cold, frightening smile. "What about it, Mr. Speeg? Do I have the right?" she asked, waving the end of the pistol around menacingly, but never moving the aim from his genital area.

"Oh, yes, ma'am."

" 'Yes, ma'am,' what?"

"You . . . uh . . . got the right to run us out of town. Come on, Hoke. Let's get out of here. There ain't nothin' worth seein' in this no'count town nohow."

Hoke and Speeg mounted their horses and rode down Center Street until they reached the edge of town. Then, urging their mounts into a gallop, they rode away quickly. Sally stayed on the buckboard, keeping an eye on them until they were well down the road. Not until then did she drive over to Longmont's.

"Why, did you ever see the man's sister?" Louis was saying, obviously in the middle of a conversation. "No wonder she isn't married. Her eyebrows alone would stop a man dead in his tracks at fifty paces."

Both Smoke and Sheriff Carson laughed at Louis's unflattering description; then, looking up, Smoke saw Sally coming in.

"Hello, Sally. All finished with your shopping, are you?" Smoke asked.

"All finished," Sally said.

"Well then, friends, I guess it's time for us to get back out to Sugarloaf," Smoke said, taking the last swallow of his beer before standing.

"We'll see you around," Sheriff Carson called.

"See you," Smoke called back as he started toward the door where Sally was waiting. "Any trouble?" he asked as he bent over to kiss her.

"Nothing I couldn't handle," Sally replied.

"That's pretty much what I figured."

Chapter Three

Stan Harbin's body was taken into Corpus Christi, where it was put on a train and shipped back to his parents in Kentucky. The other seven were brought out to the ranch, where funeral services would be conducted in the ranch chapel.

King had built the chapel before the war to accommodate the more than 150 employees of his ranch. Most, but not all, of his employees were Mexican. In fact he had once relocated an entire Mexican village, which was dying because of a prolonged drought. The relocated village, reconstructed about a quarter of a mile away, and separated from the main house by the barn, machine shed, granary, smokehouse, bunkhouse, and kitchen, consisted of more than thirty homes, identical in size and shape; all were green, with red roofs.

The residents of that village, which had the unofficial name of King's Settlement, were exceptionally loyal employees, believing, rightly, that King was their great benefactor. Babies were born there, old people died there, and gradually, the little graveyard just outside the chapel began to fill up with the departed.

Now, seven more graves were about to be added to the ranch graveyard.

Even before dawn on the day of the funeral, visitors began arriving at the ranch. Most came from Benevadis or San Diego, but many came from farther away, and those who did camped on the ranch itself. Some hadn't camped at all, but rode or drove through the night to get there.

King had thought to have a private funeral, but when the word got out that there were ten men killed in a shoot-out on the ranch, it spread throughout Duval County, as well as the neighboring counties of Nueces, Encinal, McMullen, Zapata, Starr, and Hidalgo. Some people had even come from Mexico, and many came from Corpus Christi.

There were far too many people for the chapel to hold, so priority was given to those who actually lived and worked on the ranch. The others gathered outside the chapel, content just to be there and to be present for the actual interment.

The main house, called the "Casa Grande" by the Mexican and American

55

cowboys alike, was a large, two-story edifice with a porch all the way across the front at the ground level, and an equally large balcony across the front at the second-floor level.

Richard King and Robert Kleberg were sitting on the front porch, watching as the people arrived for the funeral. Already dressed for the funeral, both men were wearing black suits with black string ties.

"What are all these people doing here?" Richard asked.

"They've come to pay their respects," Kleberg said.

"But why? I doubt that any of them ever knew any of the men that were killed," King said.

"I think they are paying their respects to you," Kleberg said.

"To me? Why on earth would they do that?"

"You are an important man in these parts," Kleberg said.

"Hrmmph," King said self-consciously.

Henrietta, King's wife, and Alice, his daughter, came out onto the front porch then. Like the men, the two women were appropriately dressed for the funeral, not only wearing black dresses, but black veils as well. Henrietta offered her arm to her husband, while Kleberg stood to take Alice's arm.

There was a large crowd gathered around outside the chapel, and as King and the others approached, they parted to make a path for them. Inside the chapel they were greeted by Padre Bustamante, the priest at the little church in Benevadis.

Bustamante took King and the others down the aisle to the front row, then held out his hand bidding them to sit. There were seven closed coffins elevated on sawhorses in front of the sanctuary.

Bustamante took his place at the front of the chapel, then began the funeral Mass.

King did not understand the Latin, so instead of listening to the words, he listened to the rhythm of the delivery. He allowed his thoughts to drift back to the war when, once before, tragedy had struck the little community of ranch workers who resided on his ranch.

Returning from a cattle-buying trip in Mexico, King discovered that twenty-three of his people had been slaughtered during a raid by the Union Army. Not only were many slaughtered, but several of the women, including the young girls, had been brutally raped.

"Who could do such a terrible thing?" he asked.

"El Carnicero," Ramon answered. At the time, Ramon had not been his foreman, but because the foreman had been one of those killed, Ramon was promoted on the spot.

"El Carnicero," King said, saying it more as if repeating it than questioning it. "The Butcher?"

"*Sí,* The Butcher," Ramon said. "Anyone who kills in such a way is a butcher."

"Are you sure he was in the Army?"

"*Sí.* He was in the Army and he carried a big sword. It is with the sword that he . . . *corte las cabezas* of the people."

He cut off the heads of the people, King thought, coming back from his reverie. Exactly like the man did who led this attack upon his ranch. Could it possibly be the same one?

King looked up toward the front of the chapel and saw that the priest was just concluding the Lord's Prayer.

"Amen" the congregation responded as one.

The seven coffins were transported outside the chapel to the adjacent cemetery. There, even those who had not been able to get into the church were able to gather around to pay their respects, and express their sorrow over the loss of so many young lives.

King stayed in the cemetery until the graveside services were concluded, and not until dirt was being shoveled onto the caskets did he, his family, and Kleberg start back to the main house.

Once Henrietta and Alice were back inside the house, King and Kleberg sat again on the chairs on the front porch. They watched as the people began leaving the funeral.

Kleberg shook his head. "Richard, we've got to do something about this."

King nodded slowly. "I know. I just don't know what yet."

"If you would like, I can go into Corpus Christi tomorrow and call in the Rangers," Kleberg said.

"No, don't do that."

"No?" Kleberg replied, surprised at the response. "Why not?"

"Well, for one thing, I think I know who did this. And if I'm right, he's making it personal."

"Who?"

"Someone that my people call The Butcher," King said. King told the story of the raid against his ranch during the war.

"It was a Regular Army unit? Not a band of guerrillas?" Kleberg asked.

"Regular Army, yes. But Major Brandt and Sergeant Stone were court-martialed and sent away to prison."

"For how long?"

"I thought, for the rest of their lives," King said. "And they may still be there. I don't know, maybe I'm just letting an active imagination get the better of me. For all I know, Brandt is still in prison . . . or dead."

"Well, then, if I go into Corpus Christi I can find out for you," Kleberg offered.

"Yes," King answered. "I think I would like that."

It was at that very moment that Alice came back out onto the porch. "Did I just hear Bob say he was going to Corpus Christi?" she asked brightly.

"Were you standing just inside the door, listening?" King asked.

"No, I was just coming out to see if you wanted coffee, and I heard Bob say he was going to Corpus Christi tomorrow. You did say that, didn't you?"

"Yes," Kleberg answered.

Alice smiled broadly. "Then this will work out just great!" she said. "Papa, you re- member a couple of weeks ago I told you I wanted to go to Austin, and you said it would be all right if I could get someone to take me to Corpus Christi to catch the train?"

"Yes, I remember," King said. "But I don't know that this is such a good time now."

"Why not?"

"Alice, you know what just happened. Do you have to ask why not?"

"Well, Papa, it didn't happen in Austin," Alice said.

Kleberg tried to hold back a laugh. "She's got you there, Richard," he said.

Despite himself, King laughed as well. "All right," he said, giving in. "You can go to Austin. How long will you be up there? Remember, we're starting the cattle drive north, and I would like for you to be back before then."

"But neither you nor Bob will actually be going on the drive, will you?"

"No, but I'd like you home before the drive starts."

"All right, Papa," Alice agreed. "I'll be visiting Loretta Dixon, and I won't stay longer than a week, I promise."

"Then, if it is all right with your mama, it's all right with me," King said.

"Oh, thank you, Papa," Alice said, kissing him on the cheek. "If you say it's all right, then Mama is a cinch."

After Kleberg put Alice on the train headed for Austin, it took only one exchange of telegrams for him to learn that Jack Brandt and Wiley Stone had been released from prison. That meant that King wasn't imagining things. It probably was Brandt who'd raided the ranch, particularly given his penchant for beheading his victims. The question was, why? Was it some sort of twisted revenge for what happened to him during the war? Since none of the cattle were stolen, Kleberg had to believe that it was something like that.

So, what now? Should Kleberg ride the forty miles back to the ranch to ask King for permission to call in the Texas Rangers? No, that would just be a waste of time. King had already made it clear that he did not want the Texas Rangers involved.

But something had to be done. The only question was, what?

Suddenly, Kleberg knew what it was, and he took it upon himself to send the next telegram. In the telegram, he asked an old friend for help.

Chapter Four

Kirby Jensen never really knew his mother, and when he was barely in his teens, he went with his father into the mountains to follow the fur trade. The pair teamed up with a legendary mountain man called Preacher. For some reason unknown even to Preacher, the mountain man took to the boy and began to teach him the ways of the mountains: how to live when others would die, how to be a man of your word, and how to fear no other living creature. On the first day they met, Preacher, whose real name was Art, gave Kirby a new name that, over the years, would become a legend in the West. After a while, even Kirby thought of himself as Smoke Jensen.

Preacher was with Smoke when he killed his first man during an Indian attack, and he took the boy in when his dying father left him in Preacher's care.[1]

Now Smoke was in his thirties, a happily

[1] *The Last Mountain Man*

married landowner whose ranch, Sugarloaf, was said to be one of the finest in the whole state. He was in the kitchen of his house, drinking coffee and leaning back against the counter, when he laughed so hard that he sprayed coffee from his nostrils.

It was a funny sight, since Smoke stood just over six feet tall and had shoulders as wide as an ax handle and biceps as thick as most men's thighs.

"I wish I had been there," Pearlie said. Pearlie was a shade under six feet tall; he was as lean as a willow branch, with a face tanned the color of an old saddle and wild, unruly black hair. His eyes were mischievous and he was quick to smile and joke, but underneath his happy demeanor was a man as hard as iron and as loyal to his friends as they come.

"Yeah, me too," Cal said. Calvin Woods was Pearlie's young friend and protégé in the cowboy life.

"I suppose if you two had been there you would have been standing over there with Smoke, staying out of it," Sally said. "Never mind that I was being accosted by two men."

"Ha! From the way I saw it, *you* were the one doing the accosting," Smoke said, laughing. "I never saw two galoots leave town so fast. I don't even think Sheriff Carson could have sent them galloping out of town the way you did."

"Miss Sally, would you really have shot him in the . . . uh," Cal began, but he was too embarrassed to finish the sentence.

"You mean his privates?" Sally asked. "You damn right I would have."

"And she wouldn't have missed either," Pearlie said. "I've seen her shoot."

"Still, I could have used a little assistance," Sally said. "It would have helped me maintain a little female decorum."

"Darlin', you've got common sense and guts," Smoke said. "That's all the female decorum you need."

"And she makes the best bear claws in Colorado," Pearlie said, reaching for one.

"Pearlie, that's your fourth," Cal said.

"Well, maybe. But I think she made them just a little smaller this time," Pearlie said as he took a bite.

Sally laughed. Her bear claws, sweet, sugarcoated doughnuts that she made by hand, were famous throughout the county, and some men had been known to ride ten miles out of their way to drop by the Sugarloaf just on the off chance she'd have a platter of them made up and cooling on the windowsill. "If you say so, Pearlie."

"They weren't no smaller," Cal argued. "They was as big as always, just like yore stomach," he added.

Sally turned around, wiping her hands on her apron. "Calvin Woods," she said, mock anger in her voice. "If you don't start using correct grammar, I'm going to have Smoke make you start taking lessons with the schoolchildren in Big Rock when school starts up again."

Pearlie grinned. "You tell him, Miss Sally."

She turned to him. "You know, your language could use a little tidying up too, Pearlie. I think listening to you talk is what has made Cal forget everything I taught him when he first came here. I don't know why I even bothered."

A couple of years after Pearlie had joined the ranch, a starving and destitute Cal, who was barely in his teens at the time, had made the mistake of trying to rob Sally of some groceries to eat. Instead of turning him over to the sheriff, she brought him home and made him one of the family along with Pearlie. Since she'd been a schoolmarm in her days before marrying Smoke, she took it upon herself to teach the wild young man grammar as well as proper manners. He'd done well at first, until Pearlie took him under his wing and began teaching him the

66

more rough and ready language and manners of cowhands. But Cal wasn't yet twenty, so Sally figured it wasn't too late to send him back to school if he needed it.

Smoke choked down another laugh until Sally turned to him. "And you, Mr. Smoke Jensen, I see you've been letting the boy smoke, and him not even out of his teens yet!"

Smoke reddened. "But Sally, Cal is doing a man's work every day and living with the other hands in the bunkhouse. It wouldn't be right to tell him to work like a man and then treat him like a little kid, would it?"

"Humph!" she snorted. "Next you'll be giving him whiskey and sending him into town to learn about women and things."

Smoke's blush deepened because Pearlie had broached just that subject with Smoke only the day before, saying that Cal was getting to that age. Smoke had suggested that Pearlie take the boy into town the next weekend and fix him up with one of the ladies who routinely dealt with that sort of malady.

"Now, darlin'," Smoke said, cutting his eyes at Pearlie and silently imploring him to keep their conversation a secret. "You know I wouldn't do any such thing."

She narrowed her eyes at him for a moment, then when she couldn't hold it in any longer she burst out laughing. "Oh, you men. You never know when you're being teased."

Smoke silently breathed a sigh of relief and changed the subject. "Speaking of town, I'm going to have to go back in today. I need a wagon load of fence posts and barbed wire for the north pasture. I don't suppose you'd like to go with me, would you?"

Sally brightened. "Just let me freshen up a bit and we'll be on our way."

"You know'd she would go with you," Cal said. "Miss Sally takes to town like my horse does to sugar cubes."

"Cal?" Sally said with raised eyebrows.

Cal looked at Sally with an anxious look on his face, wondering if he had been out of line.

"Know'd," Pearlie said quietly, prompting his younger friend.

Cal smiled. "Knew," he said, correcting himself.

Sally returned his smile. "That's better," she said.

"Pearlie, why don't you and Cal get the wagon hitched up? That is if you're through stuffing your belly," Smoke said.

"Well, truth of the matter is I kind'a noticed that Miss Sally had a fresh apple pie coolin' on the sill an' I . . ."

Smoke sighed. "You can come back and get some pie after we've left for town."

Pearlie smiled and got to his feet, letting his belt out an extra notch. "That's mighty nice of you, Smoke," he said as he grabbed his hat off a peg next to the door and pulled Cal to his feet.

"Come on, boy. Time to earn yore keep for a change."

"Me?" Cal exclaimed as he followed Pearlie out the door. "It ain't me that eats my weight in food ever' day."

"Better watch that language, Cal boy, or you're gonna be tryin' to squeeze your carcass into one of them teeny-tiny desks over at the school," Pearlie teased as they left.

Smoke walked back into the bedroom just as Sally was changing her dress. For the moment she was between dresses and she stood there in her camisole and short bloomers. The sheer lingerie showed off Sally's supple body to perfection, and Smoke took a deep breath.

"On the other hand, maybe we don't have to go into town right away," he said.

She smiled and turned to him, putting her hands on his wide shoulders. "Oh? You mean you don't really need fence posts and barbed wire?"

"No, I need them," Smoke said. "I just mean I don't need them this very minute."

"Why, Smoke Jensen, I do believe you are trying to take advantage of me," Sally teased. She leaned into him and kissed him.

Sally was as pretty, slim, and curvaceous now as she was the day they'd gotten married, and she could still make Smoke feel like a boy in his teens in the privacy of their bedroom. What's more, she made no bones about enjoying it as much as he did.

Smoke wrapped his arms around her and returned her kiss with a bit more enthusiasm. After a moment, Sally was the one who was blushing. "You'd better stop that right now, Mr. Jensen, or we aren't going to town any time soon," she murmured against his lips.

"Like I told you, there's no real hurry," Smoke replied.

"*As* I told you," Sally said, correcting him. "Sometimes your grammar is as bad as Pearlie's and Cal's."

"Oh! Pearlie and Cal!" Smoke said quickly, letting go of her and backing away. "They'll be coming back."

Sally chuckled, then pressed more tightly

against him. "You aren't going to let a little thing like that stop you, are you, coward?"

"Sally, for heaven's sake," Smoke said. "Have a little . . ." He paused, searching for the word. "Female decorum," he concluded.

Sally laughed out loud and pulled away from him. "All right, if you say so," she said.

Chapter Five

Not one for riding in a buckboard, Smoke let Sally drive the rig while he rode next to it on his big Palouse stud, Stormy. The bronc's name reflected both his personality and his coloring, which was gray with a dark-spotted white rump. Without Smoke's permission, no one could come within five feet of the horse without risking serious injury.

As he rode down the trail toward town, Smoke glanced down at Sally, recalling her playfulness in the bedroom just before they left. When it suited her to do so, Sally wore men's pants, though this morning she was wearing a dress. But no matter how she was dressed, she was never without her nickel-plated .32 revolver. She wasn't a fast-draw artist, but she was smooth with it, and she always hit where she aimed. He smiled as he thought of the two men who had accosted her yesterday. The one named Speeg didn't know how lucky he was to still have his privates. If she had wanted to, she could have taken him apart, one ball at a time.

When they reached Big Rock and rode down Main Street, many of the citizens they passed called out and waved. Part of it was because the Jensens were well known and respected in the town Smoke had helped to form, and they knew most everyone by their first names. But part of it was because of the way Sally had handled herself with the two ruffians who had accosted her. Word had spread throughout the town.

Sheriff Monte Carson was sitting on the boardwalk in front of his office with a cup of coffee in one hand and his ever-present pipe in the other. He had his chair tilted back on two legs and his feet were braced on the hitching rail in front of him.

When Smoke and Sally rode past, he raised his cup in a salute and called, "Howdy."

Smoke grinned and tipped his hat and Sally smiled and waved. "Meet you at Longmont's," Smoke said.

Carson nodded and then he pitched his coffee onto the dirt. Smoke and Monte Carson had become very good friends over the past few years. Carson had once been a well-known gunfighter, though he had never ridden the owlhoot trail.

A local rancher, Tilden Franklin, with plans to take over the county, had hired

Carson to be the sheriff of Fontana, a town just down the road from Smoke's Sugarloaf spread. When Carson learned that the man's plans were to have a sheriff who would wink at his lawlessness, he put his foot down and informed Franklin that Fontana was going to be run in a law-abiding manner from then on.

Franklin sent a bunch of his riders in to teach the upstart sheriff a lesson. The men killed Carson's two deputies and seriously wounded him, taking over the town. In retaliation, Smoke founded the town of Big Rock, and he and his band of aging gunfighters cleaned up the town of Fontana. When the fracas was over, Smoke offered the job of sheriff of Big Rock to Monte Carson. Carson married a grass widow and settled into the job like he was born to it. Neither Smoke nor the citizens of Big Rock ever had cause to regret his taking the job.

Heavyset and growing a bit of a paunch, thanks both to his wife's excellent cooking and his aversion to any real physical labor, Carson was still quick as a snake with a handgun and was as honest as a gold coin. If you obeyed the law and didn't cause any trouble in his town, you would have no trouble with him.

Down the street, Smoke dismounted and helped Sally tie the two-horse rig up to a rail in front of the general store. He went inside with her and looked around at the goods piled on tables and stacked on shelves. The store smelled of cured meat, flour, spices, candle wax, and coal oil. A large counter separated the proprietors from the customers, and on that counter was a roll of brown paper and a spool of string. Peg Johnson was behind the counter at that very moment, tending to another customer.

"Hello, Sally, Smoke," Peg said. "I'll be with you in a moment."

"No hurry," Sally said as she began looking through the dry goods.

"Uh, Sally, I'm going down to the hardware store and have Pete deliver the fence posts and wire. Then I think I'll head on over to Louis's place and drink coffee while you shop."

"All right. Do you need anything?"

"You might pick me out a couple of pair of pants and maybe some socks."

Sally smiled and fingered his shirt, which was showing some signs of wear. "I'll pick out a couple of nice shirts too, sweetheart. Can't have the master of the Sugarloaf looking threadbare, can we?"

"All right," he agreed, "but only in white or blue. None of those fancy colors you bought last time. I couldn't even give those away to Pearlie, and Lord knows, that boy has no clothes sense at all."

Sally picked up a bright red shirt with a white collar and held it up.

"How about this one?" she asked with a mischievous smile.

Smoke snorted, shook his head, and walked hurriedly out the door.

After stopping by the hardware store to take care of his business, Smoke walked down to Longmont's and, as was his custom, once inside, stepped immediately to the side and pressed his back up against the wall. He stood there a moment, letting his eyes adjust to the lower light inside while he looked for possible trouble among the patrons. Even though he knew he was almost as safe in his friend's restaurant as he was in his own house, he'd been hunted and tracked for more than half his life, and the habit of caution was so ingrained in him that he didn't even notice he was doing it.

The owner of the saloon and restaurant, Louis Longmont, was sitting at his usual table in a corner. He watched his friend go through his regular ritual upon entering the place where Louis plied his trade of gambling, which he euphemistically called "teaching amateurs the laws of chance."

Louis was a lean, hawk-faced man, with strong, slender hands, long fingers, and carefully manicured nails. He had jet-black hair and a black pencil-thin mustache. He was dressed in a black suit, with a white shirt and a crimson ascot — something he'd picked up on a trip to England some years back. He wore low-heeled boots, and a pistol hung in tied-down leather on his right side. The pistol was nickel-plated, with ivory handles, but it wasn't just for show, for Louis was snake-quick and a feared, deadly gunhand when pushed.

Although Louis was engaged in a profession that did not have a very good reputation, he was not an evil man. He had never hired his gun out for money. And while he could make a deck of cards do almost anything, he had never cheated at poker. He didn't have to cheat. He was possessed of a phenomenal memory, could tell you the odds of filling any type of poker hand, and was an expert at the technique of card counting.

Louis was just past thirty. When he was a small boy, Louis left Louisiana and came West with his parents. His parents had died in a shantytown fire, leaving the boy to cope as best he could.

Louis had coped quite well, plying his innate intelligence and willingness to take a chance into a fortune. He owned a large ranch up in Wyoming Territory, several businesses in San Francisco, and a hefty chunk of a railroad.

Though it was a mystery to many why Louis continued to stay with his saloon and restaurant in a small town, Louis explained it very simply. "I would miss it," he said. Smoke understood exactly what he was talking about.

Always the gambler, Louis once joked that he would like to draw against Smoke someday, just to see who was faster. Smoke allowed as how it would be close, but that he would win.

"You don't think that maybe I'm just a little faster?" Louis asked.

"Oh, I didn't say that," Smoke replied. "Who knows, you might be just a little faster."

"Then I don't understand. Why do you say you would win?"

"Because you are also too civilized. Your mind is distracted by visions of operas, fine foods and wines, and the odds of your winning the match. Also, your fatal flaw is that you can almost always see the good in the lowest creatures God ever made, and you refuse to believe that anyone is pure evil, without any hope of redemption."

When Louis laughed at this description of himself, Smoke continued. "I'm different. When some snake-scum draws down on me and wants to dance, my mind is clear and focused. The only thing I think about is killing the son of a bitch."

Louis never brought the issue up again.

Still standing just inside the door, Smoke glanced over and saw his friend smiling at him. He returned the grin, then moved across the floor to take a seat at Louis's table.

"Coffee?" Louis offered.

"You bet."

Louis raised a hand and said, "Andre, a cup of your best for our friend here."

Louis's French cook replied through a window into the kitchen in his thick accent, "I will give Monsieur Smoke the same coffee as everyone else, *mon ami,* and it already is the best coffee in Colorado, if not in this entire wretched country."

Both Smoke and Louis laughed. Andre was known to think the pinnacle of culture resided in Paris, France, and the opposite end of the spectrum was America, though he had been known to say a few kind words about New York City.

"I see you're still as cautious as ever when entering a room," Louis said as Andre placed a china cup and saucer in front of Smoke, and filled it from the silver service set that Louis always had on his table.

Smoke shrugged. "It's been so long it's the only way I know."

Louis sighed. He was much the same way, having made more than his share of enemies over the years. "It is hardly the most enjoyable way of living, always having to look over one's shoulder for some miscreant from one's past."

Smoke grinned. "Yes, it's a terrible way to live, but it beats the hell out of a bullet in the back."

Louis laughed. "You always have had the most succinct way of putting things in perspective, Smoke."

"So, what's been happening with you?" Smoke asked.

"Not much. Except for the little show your Sally put on for us the other day when she ran those two galoots off, the town's been as dull as dishwater. And it's been that way for the past few weeks. Why, I haven't had an interesting opponent in poker for the entire month."

"But," Smoke said, raising his eyebrows, "I'll bet that didn't keep you from taking most of their weekend pay, now, did it?"

Louis shrugged and spread his arms. "I am always willing to give lessons in the noble art of poker, even to those who will never learn from their mistakes."

Smoke was about to say that their first mistake was sitting down across a card table from Louis Longmont, when Sheriff Monte Carson ambled through the batwings.

Louis looked over and saw that Andre had seen the sheriff arrive as well, and was already bringing another cup and saucer to the table.

Carson sat down and grimaced as he pulled his chair up to the table.

"Something ailing you, Monte?" Smoke asked as he watched Carson take a deep gulp of Andre's excellent coffee.

"It's just this rheumatiz, Smoke." Carson gave a half smile. "Hell, at my age, if it don't hurt, it don't work."

"You're not all that old, Monte," Louis said, sipping his coffee with his small finger extended as if he were having high tea in Queen Victoria's garden.

"It ain't the years, Louis," Carson replied. "It's the miles, an' I got plenty of miles on this old carcass."

"Hell, I'll drink to that," Smoke said, raising his cup in a mock toast.

"How about some lunch?" Louis asked.

Smoke frowned. "I'd better wait for Sally," he said. "She's over at the general store buying clothes. That'll probably cost more than the fencing and wire I just bought."

"At least she is still interested in looking nice for you," Carson said. "My wife could wear burlap sacks and be just as happy."

Louis coughed gently. "Excuse me, gentlemen," he teased. "If you two old married gents are going to reveal all the secrets of your marriages in front of this old bachelor, I'm afraid I'm going to have to take my leave before I become terminally embarrassed."

"That'll be the day," Smoke said, laughing.

"Yeah," Carson said. "About the only time I ever seen Louis embarrassed was the time we was playing poker and he tried to bluff you with a king-high hand and you called him and beat him with a pair of deuces, Smoke."

Louis flushed. "It was the correct play," he argued, still embarrassed. "Smoke should have folded."

"That's what you get for playing with amateurs, Louis," Smoke said. "We don't always do what we are supposed to do."

"Amateur, hell," Louis said, grinning. "Give me two weeks and I could make you as good as any poker player in the country, Smoke."

"Not my game, Louis. I'm just an ordinary old rancher now."

Both Carson and Louis laughed at this.

"Yeah, you'll be an ordinary old rancher when pigs fly!" Carson said.

Just as Andre was refilling the silver service with a fresh supply of coffee, a young boy about eleven or twelve stepped hesitantly through the batwings.

Carson glanced over at him and chuckled. "Your customers are getting a mite younger here lately, Louis."

Louis raised his eyebrows at the youngster and beckoned him over to the table.

"Yes, Tommy, what is it?" he asked.

"Mr. Springer over at the telegraph office asked me to deliver this here note to Mr. Jensen," Tommy said, his eyes darting nervously toward Smoke. It was obvious that he was awestruck to be so close to the famous gunfighter.

Smoke dug in his pocket and gave the boy a dime. "Thanks," he said as he unfolded the note.

"Thank you!" Tommy exclaimed, whirling around and running from the room, already planning on just how he would spend his newfound wealth.

Smoke narrowed his eyes in thought for a moment, and then he remembered just who it was who'd sent him the telegram.

"Trouble?" Louis asked, watching his friend's face.

"Yes. It's from someone I owe a whole lot to," Smoke said. "Seems he's in some trouble and is wondering if I might be available to help him out."

"What kind of trouble?" Louis asked.

Smoke shook his head. "He doesn't say, but since he's asking for my help, I suspect it's the kind of trouble that comes out of the end of a gun."

"Just who is this hombre anyway?" Carson asked. Being a sheriff just naturally made him a suspicious sort of man.

"Bob Kleberg," Smoke answered.

Louis narrowed his eyes. "I've heard that name before, but I'm damned if I can remember where."

"He used to be the lawyer for the governor of Colorado back before we became a state," Smoke said.

Louis nodded. "Now I remember. He's the one that arranged for the governor to pardon you and Preacher before you moved up into this part of the country."

"That's right," Smoke said. "If it wasn't for him, I'd either still be on the run or I'd be rotting in a jail somewhere."

"And now he's calling in his debt?" Carson asked.

Smoke nodded. "Seems like."

"Where is this man now and what is he doing?" Louis asked.

Smoke shrugged. "The letter says he's down in Texas, near the Mexican border, and that he's running a ranch for a fellow named King. He wants me to come down there and talk about his problems and see if I can do anything to help him out."

Carson's eyes opened wide. "All the way down to the Mexican border? That must be near a thousand miles. That's a helluva long journey just to talk about something."

Smoke didn't answer, but his eyes remained on the telegram still lying on the table.

"What do you think Sally will say about you taking off on such a long trip?" Louis asked.

"Why don't you ask Sally?" a soft, feminine voice said from just behind Smoke.

Sally had entered without anyone seeing

her and was standing just to one side of the table. All the men around the table stood.

"Sally, I didn't see you come in," Smoke said, pulling out a chair for her.

Sally stepped around the table and took the chair. "What trip are you talking about?" she asked.

Ever the diplomat, Louis asked, "Would you like a cup of coffee or tea, Sally?"

"Why, thank you, Louis. I would very much appreciate a cup of Andre's wonderful coffee."

While Louis poured, Sally looked at Smoke. "Go on, dear, you were just about to tell me about the trip you are taking," she said sweetly.

"You remember that man that worked for Governor Gilpin that I told you about, the one that got me and Preacher our pardons?"

"Uh-huh," Sally said, taking her cup from Andre.

"It seems he's in a spot of trouble and he's asked me to come down to Texas and help him out of it."

"Texas?"

"Yeah, down around Corpus Christi, right near the Mexican border."

She nodded slowly. "And you feel you owe this man a debt for what he did for you and Preacher?"

Smoke shrugged. "I guess just about everything I have now is due to him in one way or another, Sally. If he hadn't gotten me my pardon, I'd never have been able to settle down and stay in one place for any length of time. I would have never even met you."

She nodded again, finished her cup of coffee, and got to her feet. "Then it's settled. We simply must go help this man out of his trouble, whatever it is."

Smoke grinned and got up also. "Sally, I knew you'd underst . . . wait a minute. Did you say *we*?"

"Yes," Sally mused as she got her purse together over her arm. "Texas should be very nice this time of the year. It's spring and the wildflowers will be blooming. As a matter of fact, I'm looking forward to going."

"But Sally," Smoke protested.

"Come along, dear," Sally said. "It's time we got home and packed for the trip."

After they'd left, Monte Carson and Louis Longmont looked at each other with open mouths.

"What a magnificent woman!" Longmont said.

Carson nodded. "Yep. She's a pistol all right."

Louis walked over to the batwings and

looked out to see Sally driving the buck-board and Smoke riding alongside as they started back toward Sugarloaf.

"Poor Smoke looks like he doesn't know what hit him," Louis said. He turned back toward Sheriff Carson, and smiled. "Can I interest you in a game of chance?"

Carson stood up quickly, again gri-macing. "Uh, no," he said. "I'd better get back to work."

"Coward," Louis challenged with a little laugh. It was clearly understood by all that the word *coward* referred only to Carson's refusal to play cards with him.

Back at the Sugarloaf, Smoke finally re-lented and quit trying to talk Sally out of making the trip with him. After all, how dangerous could it be? Whatever trouble Kleberg was in, Smoke could leave Sally in town at a nice hotel while he worked on it and she'd be perfectly safe. Besides, he could take Cal and Pearlie with him, and if there were any serious trouble in the region, he could have them watch Sally while he concentrated on the bad guys and extri-cating Kleberg from whatever jam he'd gotten himself into.

They made arrangements to take the train to Corpus Christi, and Smoke decided to bring their horses and extra gear with them by renting an entire cattle car. He had no idea what kind of mounts would be available that far south, but he knew he could depend on the big Palouse studs when the chips were down.

Chapter Six

Concepcion sat baking in the sun like a lizard on a hot rock, its dirt-colored adobe buildings rising from the ground as if they were an occurrence of nature, rather than man-made. The little village was built in a square around the Catholic church, which, as in most of the little Mexican villages in this part of Texas, was the most prominent building. A well in the center square provided water for the entire town. When Brandt and his riders came to within a mile of the town, he held up his hand to halt his troops.

"There it is," he said. "Concepcion."

"You'll pardon me for sayin' so, Major, but that sure don't look like much of a town to me," Stone said.

"It's just right for our purposes," Brandt replied. "It'll have food, water, liquor, and whores to keep the men occupied. And it's far enough away from King's ranch so as not to be discovered accidentally, but close enough that it will be real easy for us to get down there, do our business, then leave. This will be our headquarters."

"What about the sheriff?"

"You're looking at the sheriff," Brandt said.

"You?" Stone asked in surprise. "You are the sheriff?"

Brandt took his canteen from his pommel, then pulled the cork.

"Not yet, but I soon will be," he answered, just before turning the canteen up to take a drink.

Two children were squatting on the edge of town. A scorpion was between them, and they were teasing the creature, laughing every time the scorpion's tail would lash toward the sticks they were holding. One of the children saw the riders approaching, and he pointed. It was so unusual to see this many riders that he and his friend both stood to examine this phenomenon more closely. They forgot about their game with the scorpion, and the venomous arachnid scampered off to safety the moment its two tormentors were distracted.

By the time Brandt and his men reached the edge of town, several of its 107 residents, more than half of whom were Mexican, had learned of the arrival, either by the shouts of others, or in some cases by the sound of hoofbeats from the sixty horses. In pairs and small groups, they left their homes and places of business to watch in interest, and some anxiety, as the riders approached. There had not been this many riders coming through town since the war, and because these men were riding in the same, orderly formation, some wondered if another war had begun.

The Catholic priest, Padre Julio Gonzales, came out of his little church and stood at the side of the well, watching the riders arrive, wondering how their arrival might affect his people. The riders came all the way into the center square before Brandt held up his hand.

"Troop, halt!" he called.

His men, riding in a well-maintained military column of twos, stopped. The little cloud of dust that had accompanied their entrance into the town, drifted away on the hot breath of air.

Padre Gonzales hurried out to address the obvious leader of the riders.

"Puedo ayudar, señor?"

"What?"

"I am sorry, excuse the Spanish. I asked if I may be of some help."

"Sergeant, dismiss the men," Brandt said.

Stone stood in the stirrups and looked back over the men.

"Troop dismissed!" he called.

The men, who until that moment had been as disciplined as any army, let out a yell, dismounted, and started moving toward the two drinking establishments in town, one Mexican cantina and one American saloon.

Brandt walked over to the well, where a half-filled bucket and dipper sat on the stone wall that encircled the well. Scooping up water with the dipper, he took off his hat and poured it over his head. As it cascaded down, it left rivulets in the trail dirt that was caked over him.

He turned the second scoop of the dipper up to his mouth, and took a deep, Adam's-apple-bobbing drink, with water pouring from the edge of the cup and running down his chin and onto his shirt. Not until his thirst was slaked did he respond to the padre's question.

"Yeah, you can help me," he said. "Has this town got a sheriff?"

The padre's face brightened into a smile. If the stranger was looking for the sheriff, then he couldn't mean them any harm.

"Sí, el sheriff. Su oficina está ahí."

93

"Speak American, you pig-faced bastard," Brandt ordered.

The smile left the padre's face and with an expression of hurt and controlled anger, he pointed to the sheriff's office.

"Come with me," Brandt said to Stone. As they started toward the building the padre had pointed out, they heard a woman scream, and a man shouting curses.

"*Ésa es mi esposa!* That is my wife! What are you doing, Señor?"

The man's protest was cut short by a blow to his head from a pistol barrel.

"Sounds like the men are beginning to get settled in," Stone said with an evil chuckle.

Without a second thought as to what the men might be doing, Brandt and Stone continued toward a low-lying adobe building that had a sign over a door reading LA OFICINA DE SHERIFF, and another sign that read SHERIFF'S OFFICE.

Brandt drew his sword, looked over at Stone, and nodded. Stone drew his pistol, then kicked the door open.

"*Qué es esto?*" the sheriff shouted, standing up from behind his desk. His deputy stood up as well.

"A change of command," Brandt said, whipping his sword around. The sheriff's severed head bounced on the desk, then fell to the floor. The headless body fell back-ward gushing blood from a truncated neck.

"Madre de Dios!" the deputy said, looking on in shock. It was the last thing he ever said because Stone shot him dead.

"Find the undertaker," Brandt said. "Have him get these bodies out of here." Brandt sat down behind the desk, then put his feet up. "This will be our command post," he said.

Despite its Spanish name, which meant Red Cat, the Gato Rojo was the American saloon in the small town. And while others in the town were frightened by the sudden appearance of so many Americans, Carl Kunz was doing a booming business. Right now nearly forty men were crowded into his place of business, standing at the bar, or sitting at the tables. To Kunz's delight, they ordered food, drink, and from time to time, took one of the women into the little lean-to room at the back of the building.

In the time Brandt had been here, he and his men had taken over the town. The women of the town were staying in their homes, too frightened to go out into the street. Those who did go out were literally taking their lives into their own hands, especially today, because two of Brandt's men were standing at the batwing doors of the Gato Rojo, taking potshots at anyone who ventured onto the street. They weren't trying to kill them. They were just coming as close to them as they could, without hitting them.

One of the men fired.

BANG!

"Ha! Did you see that son of a bitch jump? I'll bet you he crapped in his pants."

"You weren't all that close," the other one said. "Watch this."

BANG!

The sound of a gunshot filled the saloon.

Kunz moved from one end of the long, rough-hewn bar to the other, answering the demands of the men as they ordered beer, tequila, or whiskey. He knew that he should resent them for being in his town and frightening his neighbors the way they were. He knew, also, that they had burglarized some of the stores in town, just taking what they wanted. But for some reason, here in the saloon, they were paying for their goods and services, including even the whores. And Kunz got one half of what the whores got. Maybe it was wrong of him, but realistically, what could he do? He was just one man. There was no way he could stand up to

96

them. So, if they were willing to pay him for his services, what was the harm?

BANG!

More laughter from the two men standing at the front door.

The leader of the group, Jack Brandt, was a large man with long black hair, a black beard, and a scar that cut through, but did not obliterate, his right eye. He insisted upon being called Major. Brandt's second in command was Wiley Stone, and he was called Sarge.

Though they had taken over the sheriff's office, both Brandt and Stone seemed to spend most of their time right here, in the Gato Rojo saloon.

Sitting at the table with Brandt and Stone were Brad Preston, Three-Finger Bill Manning, and a young tough who called himself Waco Jones.

"Hey, Kunz," Stone called. "Bring me over a jar of them pickled pig's feet."

"Yes, sir, Sarge, right away," Kunz replied. Kunz brought over a jar and sat it on the table. Stone stuck his hand down into the vinegar and pulled out a pinkish-white pig's foot, then began gnawing on it.

BANG!

"What the hell are they shooting at?" Manning asked.

"Ah, don't get so jumpy," Preston said. "They're just havin' a little fun." He watched Stone as he continued to gnaw on the pig's foot. "How you can eat them pig's feet is beyond me."

Stone merely smiled at him, took another bite, and smacked his lips in exaggerated appreciation.

"It damn near makes me sick just to look at you," Preston said.

"That's 'cause you never tried them," Waco said. "Hell, I think they're good. Fact is, I think I'll have me one myself." Waco stuck his hand down in the jar.

"How the hell would you know what's good? You're still wet behind the ears," Preston teased. "What are you now? Seventeen? Eighteen?"

"I'm eighteen," Waco said.

"Tell me, Waco. How old was you when you had your first woman?" Preston asked. "Or have you even had yourself a woman yet?"

"I'm not sure how old I was when I had my first woman, but I know that I killed my first man when I was fifteen," Waco answered. He smiled at Preston, but it wasn't a smile of mirth. "I killed the son of a bitch for raggin' me," he added pointedly.

"Here, that's enough of that," Brandt

said. "We have plenty of enemies without. We don't need enemies within."

BANG!

"I wasn't fightin'," Preston said. "And I didn't mean nothin' by it. I was just havin' a little fun, that's all."

"I don't like that kind of fun," Waco said.

"Hey, Major," Stone said. "You reckon King has figured out yet that it's us that hit him?"

"I doubt it," Brandt said. "I don't think King is all that smart."

"He must be a little smart," Manning said.

The others glared at him.

"I mean . . . to have a ranch that big," Manning said. "He'd have to be a little smart for that, wouldn't you think?"

"Havin' it is one thing," Brandt said. "Keepin' it is another. And by the time we get through with that son of a bitch, he won't have two coppers to rub together."

BANG!

"Hey, Major, what you got against this here feller King anyway?" Waco asked.

"Do you know who King is?" Brandt asked.

"Yeah, sure I know who he is. He is Captain Richard King, and he owns a big ranch," Waco said. "But that don't tell me what you got against him."

"Tell him, Stone," Brandt ordered

Stone had just taken a drink of beer, and flecks of foam were hanging in his mustache. He used his sleeve to wipe them away.

"You wasn't with us durin' the war," Stone said.

"Hell, Sarge, ain't nobody in this here whole bunch was with you then, but you'n the major," Manning said. "And Waco here was so young then that he was still pissin' in his pants."

"Yes, well, this man Captain King is the selfsame son of a bitch who got the major and me put in prison," Stone said. "And we was doin' no more than our duty. I mean, the son of a bitch was feedin' the Confederate Army. That made him a legal target for our raid, far as I'm concerned. Only the guv'ment didn't see it that way, and the reason they didn't see it that way was because King is such a rich bastard, he bought 'em off."

BANG! "Ha!" one of the men at the front door shouted. "Did you see that? I knocked his hat off his head!"

"So what. Them Mexs wear big hats," the other shooter said.

"Well, hell, Major, if you got somethin' against him, why don't we just kill him?" Waco asked, continuing the conversation at the table. "You want me to kill him? I'll kill him for you."

"Oh, don't you worry about that. We're goin' to kill him, all right," Brandt said. "But not until we break him. I want him to die a poor man."

"What's our next move?" Manning asked.

"We need to raise a little cash," Brandt said. "I figure the next time we go back to Captain King's ranch, we'll cut out about two hundred head. One of the reasons I chose this town as our headquarters is that it is very close to the Mexican border and I've found a man who will pay us ten dollars a head for all the cattle we can bring to him."

"Ten dollars a head?" Preston asked. "Hell, Major, they're paying three times that up in Kansas."

"And when they start the herd to Kansas, we'll go along with them," Brandt said. "But in the meantime, we need some operating money. Unless you have a couple thousand dollars you want to throw into the pot."

BANG!

"I ain't got no money," Preston said. "Leastwise, nothin' like that. All I got is about ten dollars."

"Then we will take the money where we can get it. Unless, maybe, you think you can run this outfit better than I can."

"You're the boss, Major," Preston said nervously. "I didn't mean nothin' by what I said. I was just talkin', that's all."

Like more than half of the men who were riding with Brandt, Preston had been in prison with him, though Preston had served only five years, while Brandt and Stone had each served over fifteen years.

One of the two girls of the house came over to their table then. She couldn't have been much over thirty-five, though the dissipation of her profession made her look much older. She was somewhat chubby, with stringy, unkempt hair. A couple of years ago a drunken customer had knocked out two of her teeth, giving her a gap-toothed smile. She was wearing a very low-cut camisole, over which spilled an overly generous pair of breasts.

BANG!

"Oh!" the woman said, jumping.

Preston and the others at the table laughed. "What's the matter, Becky? You lettin' a little thing like a gunshot scare you?"

"It does make me nervous," Becky admitted.

"No need in bein' nervous about it, unless you the one gettin' shot at. Where you been anyhow? I haven't seen you all afternoon."

"I've been asleep."

"Asleep? In the middle of the day?"

"Well, honey," Becky said seductively. "You boys rode me pretty hard last night, then you put me away wet."

"Son of a bitch, Becky, how you talk," Manning said as he grabbed himself.

"So, how about it? Are any of you ready to show ole Becky a good time?"

Preston chuckled. "Well, now, that's the problem, Becky. Seems to me that I show you a better time than you show me. Hell, maybe I should charge you."

The others at the table laughed.

"Hoo, now, ain't you the one, though?" Becky teased. "Well, don't you worry none. If you ain't ready for me just yet, they's plenty others in here that is."

BANG!

"Oh, shit!" one of the men at the front door said.

Brandt looked toward the door. "What do you mean, 'Oh, shit'?" he called. "What happened, Lou?"

"I shot the son of a bitch," Lou said, his gun still smoking.

"Dead?"

"Yeah, I think so." Lou looked back at Brandt. "It was an accident, Major. I didn't mean to kill 'im."

"Get out there and take care of it."

"Take care of it? How? What do you mean, take care of it?"

"You can't leave him lyin' in the street. I'm not goin' to run a town that has bodies lyin' in the street."

"Well, hell, don't you think some Mex is goin' to pick 'im up?"

"I said you take care of it," Brandt said. "Take him down to the undertaker."

"All right," Lou said reluctantly. "You come with me, Al."

"What the hell for? You're the one killed him."

" 'Cause I can't carry him by myself."

"Go with him, Al," Brandt ordered.

"All right, Major, if you say so. But it don't seem fair to me, seein' as I'm not the one that shot the son of a bitch."

As the two men left, Brandt looked up at Preston. "I want you to go into Corpus Christi tomorrow and meet someone that's coming in on the train."

"All right. What's his name?"

"Pugh," Brandt said. "Dingus Pugh. He was in prison with us. You remember him, don't you?"

"Oh, yeah, I remember him."

"I told him he could join up with us, but I need someone to meet him and tell him where we are."

"Sure, I'll do it," Preston said. "I'll be glad to." He smiled broadly. "I'm always ready to go into Corpus Christi."

"Yeah, I thought you would be," Brandt replied.

Chapter Seven

Alice King enjoyed her trip to Austin. When she was younger, she had attended finishing school in Austin and, while there, met Loretta Dixon, the daughter of a state senator. The two young women became fast friends, and had been exchanging letters and occasional visits ever since.

Although Alice loved the ranch, she did sometimes miss some of the things she had enjoyed while attending school in Austin. Austin had theaters and operas and fine restaurants, to say nothing of the excitement of its just being the state capital, where one could attend sessions of the senate or the assembly and watch the state government in action.

But even more than the cultural aspects of the city, she always enjoyed the opportunity of visiting with a girlfriend her own age. Although she lived in luxury on the ranch, she was somewhat isolated, so she very much enjoyed the opportunity of being around another young woman of her own age and approximate social station.

What she particularly liked was being able to discuss very personal things with Loretta, and during this trip she had told her all about Bob Kleberg. They laughed as they made plans for her wedding.

On the last day of her visit, Loretta's mother gave an afternoon tea to honor Alice. To Alice's surprise, she was somewhat of a celebrity, due to the fact that her father's ranch was so large and so well known.

"Is it true that it would take one entire day just to ride from one side of the ranch to the other?" one of the girls asked.

"Oh, I think it would take longer than that," Alice said. "It is about the same distance across the ranch as it is from New York to Philadelphia."

"It is larger than the entire state of Rhode Island," Loretta pointed out.

Alice was uncomfortable with such conversation because it seemed to her that it could be construed as bragging. But the young women who had come to the party were so fascinated by it all that they continued to ply her with questions, so she answered as well as she could.

"How did such a ranch come to be?" one of the young women asked.

"Well, it was started in 1853," Alice explained, "after Papa traveled north from Brownsville to attend the Lone Star Fair in Corpus Christi. His route took him through the Wild Horse Desert, where he ran across the Santa Gertrudis Creek, the first live water he had seen in one hundred twenty-four miles. According to Papa, the creek was an oasis shaded by large mesquite trees, and it offered protection from the sun, as well as cool, sweet water to refresh the traveler. He said he fell in love with the place at that very moment and vowed to find out who owned the land so he could buy it."

"You mean someone else owned that whole big ranch?"

Alice laughed. "No. He just bought the land around the creek, then began adding to it until it became what it is today."

"Which is the largest and finest ranch in Texas," a man's voice said, and all the women looked around to see Senator Dixon, Loretta's father. "I hate to spoil your party, ladies, but Alice has to catch a train tonight. Alice, my carriage is waiting."

"Thank you," Alice said.

"I'll ride down to the depot with you," Loretta offered.

The sun was just going down as Alice and Loretta were driven toward the depot. A matched team pulled the Victorian carriage smartly through the lengthening shadows, their way lighted by lanterns at the front and rear. The driver halted at the edge of the depot, then napped on his seat while the two young women in the back continued their conversation.

"You will be sure to invite me to the wedding, won't you?" Loretta asked.

"Of course I will. Why, I intend for you to be my maid of honor," Alice said.

"Pink," Loretta said. "All the bridesmaids must wear pink. I look good in pink."

"Then pink it is." Suddenly Alice laughed.

"What is it?"

"Poor Bob," she said. "Here, we have the wedding all planned out, even to the color of the bridesmaids' dresses, and he doesn't even know yet that we are getting married."

"Well, what he doesn't know won't hurt him," Loretta said, and both girls laughed uproariously.

A distant whistle got their attention.

"Oh," Alice said. "The train is coming. I guess it really is time to say good-bye."

"Did you take a room?" Loretta asked.

"No, it is just an overnight trip. I'll be there shortly after breakfast in the morning. A berth in the Pullman car is all I need."

★ ★ ★

Because it was dark when the train pulled out of the station, Alice had the porter make up her berth right away. She was in bed within half an hour and, partly because she was tired from so much activity during the week, and partly because of the relaxing rhythm of the train, Alice was asleep quickly. She slept soundly all through the night.

Had Alice ridden in a parlor car, she would have met the Jensens. For, in addition to chartering a cattle car for his stock, Smoke Jensen had taken two rooms in the Wagner Parlor Car, one for him and Sally, and one for Cal and Pearlie. The center of the car was, as the name indicated, a parlor, richly paneled and carpeted, and with over-stuffed seats that could swivel to allow passengers to look out at the passing scenery or face inside for conversation.

At one end of the parlor area a large, silver-plated coffee urn sat on a serving table. A tray of pastries sat beside the coffee urn. Pearlie walked up to the table and took two of the pastries.

"Damn, Pearlie," Cal said. "You had enough breakfast this morning to choke a horse, and now that's about the fifth time you've been back to get yourself some of them sweets. You plannin' on eatin' all of 'em?"

Pearlie had just taken a large bite from one, and with flakes of powdered sugar on his lips, he looked out at the others in the car.

"Uhm . . . anyone else want one?" he asked, though the words were muffled.

When nobody answered, he looked back at Cal. "No sense in lettin' 'em go to waste," he said.

"I would say that you are going to spoil your dinner," Cal said, "but that would be a laugh. Nothing kills your appetite."

Sally was reading *Harper's Weekly* magazine, and from time to time, as she came upon something interesting, she would share it with Smoke.

"Smoke, have you ever seen a telephone?" Sally asked.

"No, I can't say as I have," Smoke said. "But I've heard of them."

"What about Mr. Edison's talking machine?"

Smoke nodded. "Well, yes, I did see one of them in Denver."

"Well, listen to this smart idea." She began reading. "It is still not clear as to what purpose Mr. Edison's talking machine will be put, but what if some clever scientist could find a way to connect it to the telephone? Then, if someone engaged the instrument to contact the house of a subscriber who was absent, Mr. Edison's talking machine could answer the telephone and record a message that the subscriber could retrieve at a later time."

Finishing the reading, Sally looked up at Smoke. "We do live in a marvelous age."

"I'd like to have me one of them telly-phones," Cal said.

"What would you do with it?" Pearlie asked.

"Why, if I wanted to go for a walk or a ride with a pretty girl, I would just call her on the tellyphone," Cal said. " 'Hello,' I'd say. 'This here is Calvin Woods. Would you like to go ridin' with me this afternoon? You would? Well, fine, I'll be by for you at two o'clock.' " Cal smiled broadly. "See how easy that would be?"

"Yeah," Pearlie snickered. "And it would be just that much easier for her to tell you no."

The conductor came through the car then, and Smoke called out to him.

"How much longer until we reach Corpus Christi?"

The conductor pulled his watch from his

pocket, snapped it open, and examined the face.

"Oh, I'd say less than half an hour now," he said.

It had been a four-day run down from Big Rock, and though the car had been comfortable, it was good to hear that the trip was nearly over.

Smoke got up to stretch, then reached for his hat.

"Where are you going?" Sally asked, looking up from her magazine. "He said we have half an hour yet."

"I know, but I thought I'd just go back and check on the livestock one last time. I'll be right back."

"Want me to go with you, Boss?" Pearlie asked.

"No need."

Five years ago, Private Dingus Pugh went absent without leave from Ft. Clark, Texas, riding an Army horse and carrying an Army pistol. He was arrested when he tried to sell the horse in San Antonio, was court-martialed, and was sentenced to five years in prison.

While in prison he met Jack Brandt and Wiley Stone. When Brandt got out of prison, which was three months before

113

Pugh's sentence was to end, he recruited Pugh for his army.

"Why would I want to join your army when I ran away from the one I was already in?" Dingus asked.

"You can get rich in my army," Brandt had answered. "Can you get rich in the one you were in?"

The idea that he could get rich appealed to him, so Pugh agreed and was given instructions by Brandt on where to find him. Brandt was turned out of jail with a new pair of blue jeans, a flannel shirt, and five dollars. Five dollars was not enough money to buy a train ticket to where he wanted to go, so Pugh augmented his purse by breaking into a store and stealing sixty-three dollars.

Now he was sitting in the dining car nursing a second cup of coffee as he ogled a beautiful girl at her breakfast. That was one thing about prison. There were no women. And having only been out for two days, he really hadn't had the opportunity to meet one. But his luck had just changed, and he intended to meet this one.

When she finished her breakfast and left, Dingus left as well, hurrying after her. He caught up with her on the second vestibule.

"Hold it, miss," he called. "You dropped something."

★ ★ ★

All the while Alice was at her breakfast, she had been aware of the man staring at her. It had been unpleasant, but because they were both in a public place she had not let it worry her. But being confronted here on the vestibule between cars was a little disconcerting. She started into the next car, but before she could reach the door he leaped across the vestibule plates and stood in her way. In fact, he was now standing in such a way so as to force her to the side of the vestibule, blocking her from going forward or returning to the car she had just left. She could smell the smoke from the engine, and feel the wind against her. The vestibule plates shook and rattled under her feet, and the car wheels clacked as they passed over the rail joints.

"What do you want?" she asked in a frightened tone.

"I told you, you dropped something," the man said.

"No, I don't think I did."

The man held up a ten-dollar bill. "You dropped this here money."

"No, I didn't. If you found it, someone else must've dropped it."

"But I seen you drop it," the man said. He smiled at her, showing a mouth of crooked, yellowed teeth. "You ain't callin' ole Dingus a liar now, are you, missy? That wouldn't be very nice now, would it?"

"Then, if I dropped it, you may have it," Alice said. "Please, just go on and let me return to my seat."

"I tell you what, missy. I seen that there was a stock car back there. There's bound to be some soft hay. What say me'n you go on back there? You show Dingus a good time, and this here ten dollars is yours. Now that's a lot more'n I'd have to give to any saloon doxy."

"What? Sir! How dare you make such a proposition to me?"

Dingus pulled his pistol out of his holster, pointed it at her, and covered it with his hat. "Here's the thing, little lady," he said. "You're goin' to go back to that stock car with me whether you take the ten dollars or not. 'Cause if you don't, I'm goin' to shoot you right here and throw you off the train."

"You . . . you wouldn't dare!" Alice said. "You would never get away with it!"

"Oh, yes, I would," he said. "As much noise as these here trains make, nobody would even hear the gunshot. Now, what do you say? Are you goin' to come back with me?"

★ ★ ★

At that moment, Smoke Jensen stepped out onto the vestibule. Seeing a man and woman there, he smiled at them.

"Good morning," he said.

"Mornin'," the man replied. "Say good morning to the man, Martha."

There was something about the woman's face that alerted Smoke.

"Good morning," the woman said in a small, choked voice.

Nodding, Smoke stepped on by them, and into the next car.

"Well, now, you handled that just fine, Martha," Dingus said, laughing. "Now, let's . . . uhh!"

That was as far as he got, because Smoke came back out of the car, grabbed Dingus by the scruff of the neck and the seat of his pants, ran him toward the edge of the vestibule, and shoved him off, pushing him hard enough that he cleared the car.

"Ahhh!!!" Dingus shouted, but his shout quickly faded as the train moved on.

Smoke turned back toward the woman, who had watched the entire scene in shock.

"How . . . how did you know?" she asked.

"I saw that he was holding a gun under his hat, and it was pointed at you. I didn't make a mistake, did I? You didn't welcome his company, did you?"

Alice shook her head. "No, sir, I assure you, you did not make a mistake. I did not welcome his company, and I thank you."

Smoke nodded, and touched the brim of his hat.

"I'm glad I could be of service," he said before he stepped back into the car.

Captain Richard King, his wife, Henrietta, and Robert Kleberg were sitting in the restaurant of the Hotel Peabody in Corpus Christi, the remains of a late breakfast on the table before them. From the large window in front of the restaurant, they had a magnificent view of the bay. Several ships were tied up at the docks, almost equally divided between sailing ships and steam vessels. Some of the ships belonged to King and when they had come into town the day before, he had met with a few of his captains, as well as with the man who ran his operation out of an office in Corpus Christi.

He had also exchanged telegrams with cattle buyers in Dodge City.

"The going rate right now is thirty-two dollars per head," King said. "And they expect that price to hold through the next three months."

"Ten thousand head," Kleberg said, "with an anticipated attrition rate of twelve percent, should return two hundred eighty-one thousand and six hundred dollars."

King smiled. "Not a bad payday for someone who started his working career at six dollars a month, is it?"

Kleberg chuckled. "No, sir, it's not bad at all," he said.

"Oh, did you check on the train?"

"Yes, it's on time," Kleberg said.

King looked over at his wife. "Well, Mrs. King, what do you think? Do you think your daughter enjoyed her visit?"

"Oh, I'm sure Alice had a good time in Austin," Henrietta replied. "But I am so glad that she is coming back. I've really missed her." Looking over at Kleberg, she smiled. "And I suspect I'm not the only one who is glad she is coming back."

Kleberg ducked his head slightly. "No, ma'am," he said. "You aren't the only one who is glad she's coming back."

King pulled his watch and looked at it. "Well, if the train is on time, like you say, it should be here very soon. Shall we go down to the depot?"

"If you are asking me, I say yes," Henrietta said.

"Richard, uh, wait," Kleberg said as King started to get up.

The tone of Kleberg's voice and the expression on his face alerted King to something, and he sat back down. "What is it?" King asked.

"Before we go, there's something I need to tell you," Kleberg said.

"Oh? What's that?"

"Don't tell me Alice missed the train," Henrietta said anxiously.

"No, no, nothing like that," Kleberg said quickly. "I'm sorry if I caused you concern. It's just that someone else is coming on the train."

"Someone else? Who?"

"Please forgive me for my secrecy," Kleberg said. "But I would rather wait until he is here."

King chuckled. "All right," he said. "I suppose I can wait to find out."

The depot platform was a bustle of activity when the train pulled into the station. There were those who were waiting to leave on the train, those who were meeting the arriving passengers, and many more who had no purpose other than to just watch the train come and go.

Vendors plied their wares among the

waiting crowd, among them an old Mexican woman. She was wrinkled and humped over, and her chin extended forward and her nose hooked downward so that it looked as if nose and chin could join. She worked quickly, and with deft fingers, assembling the spicy ingredients of a taco. Wrapping the taco in a piece of newspaper, she handed it to her customer in exchange for a coin.

"Here it comes!" someone shouted, and in the distance they could hear the train whistle. A few minutes later, the train rolled into the station, its huge driver wheels pounding against the track as wisps of steam feathered out from the drive cylinders. The train squeaked to a halt, then sat there, venting steam as if it were the labored breathing of some exhausted beast of burden. The gearboxes on the car wheels popped and snapped as they cooled.

"Oh, there she is!" Henrietta called excitedly when she saw Alice step down from the train. "Alice!" she called. "Alice, we're over here!"

Alice embraced her mother first, then her father, and finally, with an embarrassed smile, Kleberg.

"Oh," Alice said. "They are beginning to unload the baggage car. I bought some lovely things while I was in Austin. I am going to go keep an eye on them to see that they don't destroy anything."

"I'll come with you, dear," Henrietta said, walking away with her daughter.

Standing among the crowd, awaiting the train, was Brad Preston. Dispatched by Brandt to meet Dingus Pugh, he watched the passengers as they stepped down from the train. Three-Finger Manning and Waco Jones had come to Corpus Christi with him, but neither one had come down to the depot.

"You're the only one can recognize him," Waco said. "You was the one that was with him in prison. Me'n Three-Finger will be waitin' for you in one of the saloons. When your friend gets here, come get us and we'll have a drink or two before we get started back."

Preston would have argued back, but he knew that what Waco was saying was right.

When he didn't see Dingus get off the train, he walked over to speak to the conductor.

"Is ever'one off that's supposed to be off?" he asked.

"Why do you ask?"

"I was lookin' to meet someone, an' he didn't get off."

"Well, you might try toward the front of the train," the conductor suggested. "Some of the passengers in the parlor car were coming here, and they may still be gathering their things before detraining."

Preston laughed. "This here fella ain't likely to be ridin' in no parlor car," he said. "Maybe he missed the train. When's the next one down from Austin?"

"I believe there will be another one to-night at midnight."

"All right, I reckon I can wait on it," Preston said. "I'll just go have me a few drinks before then."

As Preston walked away from the depot, he didn't glance toward the four people who had just gotten down from the parlor car. If he had, he might have recognized Smoke Jensen as the man with whom he had had a run-in back in Colorado about ten years earlier.

There were twelve saloons in Corpus Christi, and Preston looked through half of them before he found Manning and Waco Jones. Even though it was not yet noon, both men were drunk.

Chapter Eight

Like Preston, Kleberg had watched the passengers detrain without seeing who he was looking for.

"What about this mysterious person you are looking for?" King asked. "Have you seen him yet?"

"No, sir," Kleberg answered. "Not yet."

At that moment, Kleberg looked toward the front of the train and saw Smoke Jensen leading a horse down a ramp from the attached stock car. He smiled.

"There he is," Kleberg said.

"There who is?"

"Toward the front of the train. You see the fella leading the horse down the ramp?"

By now, there were three men leading horses down the ramp.

"Which one?"

"The one in front," Kleberg said.

"Yes, I see him. What about him?"

"That's Smoke Jensen."

"Smoke Jensen?" King asked. "Wait a

minute. Do you mean *the* Smoke Jensen? The famous gunfighter?"

"Yes."

"Well, it would be interesting to meet him, I suppose," King said. "I mean, I've certainly heard a lot about him over the years. But I'm curious. How did you happen to know he would be on this train?"

"Because I sent for him," Kleberg said.

"You *sent* for him?"

"Yes."

"I don't understand. Why would he come just because you sent for him?"

"He owes me a big, big favor," Kleberg replied.

"And that brings me to my second question. Why did you send for him?"

"I figured he could help us with our . . . uh . . . problem," Kleberg said.

King let out a sigh, then put his hand on Kleberg's shoulder.

"Look, Bob, I know you did what you think is right. But I don't want to do that."

"You don't want to do what?"

"I don't want to use a hired gun to take care of my problem."

"Richard, he's not exactly a hired gun. As far as I know, he's never actually hired his guns out to anyone. Besides that, he is a wealthy man in his own right. I doubt that

125

he would take any money for his services, even if you offered it to him."

"Then what would make him get involved?"

"I told you, he owes me a favor. And he has a very strong sense of what is right and what is wrong."

"He sounds like an admirable man."

"He is, Richard. He is one of the finest men I've ever met."

"Then that makes me all the sorrier that you didn't check with me first. I hate putting an honorable man through all this. But I can't use him, Bob. I just feel that it would only make matters worse."

"All right," Kleberg said, obviously disappointed by King's pronouncement. "I'll go talk to him, and tell him that it was all a mistake, that we won't be needing him after all."

"I'm sorry, Bob. I just . . . well, I just wish you had checked with me first, that's all."

"No, sir, I'm the one should be sorry," Kleberg said. "I clearly overstepped my bounds on this, and I've put myself in an awkward position. I've no one but myself to blame."

As Kleberg started toward the train, he saw a fourth horse being led down the ramp by a very pretty woman, and realized that she, like the two young men, was with

Smoke. That was going to make it even more difficult for him to tell Smoke that he wouldn't need him after all.

Smoke looked up as Kleberg approached, then smiled and stuck out his hand.

"It's been a long time, but unless I'm wrong, you are Mr. Kleberg," he said.

"I am. But please, call me Bob," Kleberg replied.

"Sally, I want you to meet Bob Kleberg. I owe him a lot . . . my life, practically, because if it hadn't been for him, why, I would never even have gotten to meet you," Smoke said. "Bob, this is my wife Sally."

"I'm very pleased to meet you, ma'am," Kleberg said.

"And I, you," Sally said. "Smoke has told me many times how you arranged for the pardon for him and Preacher."

"Yes, well, I'm glad I could do it. They were good men, being unjustly pursued," Kleberg said.

"And this is Pearlie and Cal," Smoke said. "No-accounts, the both of them," he said, though his broad smile showed that he was teasing. "But they are my friends nevertheless. And since I don't know exactly what you have in mind for me to do, I figured having these two along would be to my advantage."

"I, uh," Kleberg started. He coughed, and scratched the side of his face. "Well, the truth is . . . uh . . ."

"What is it?" Smoke asked.

"Yes, well, the truth is, turns out I brought you down here for nothing."

"Oh? You mean the problem has resolved itself?"

"No, not exactly," Kleberg said. He pulled on his collar. "Uh, Mr. King doesn't want to use any hired guns."

Smoke nodded. "I can understand that," he said. "But we're not exactly hired guns. I'm not here for money. I came down to repay a favor for a friend. And any friend of a friend is my friend."

"It's not the money, it's the idea of bringing in outside guns." Kleberg ran his hand through his hair. "I'm sorry," he said. "I'm really very sorry."

Upon seeing the difficulty Kleberg was having in telling him, Smoke broke into a wide, easy smile.

"Don't worry about it," Smoke said. "We'll spend a few days in town, look around and enjoy the sights, then go back home. We've been needing a vacation anyway."

After they got rooms in a hotel and had lunch, Sally decided she would like to spend the afternoon shopping. Cal offered to go with her to carry any packages. Smoke said he would check out some of the local saloons and Pearlie decided to go with him.

Smoke and Pearlie were standing at the bar of the Boar's Head Saloon at about mid-afternoon when the batwing doors slapped open and a young man stepped in. He was scratched and bruised, and his clothes were dirty and torn. When he saw Smoke standing at the bar, he let out a loud yell.

"You!" he shouted, pointing at Smoke. "You threw me off the train, you son of a bitch!"

The intensity of the yell brought all conversation in the saloon to a halt as everyone looked toward the angry young man standing in front of the door.

Slowly, Smoke turned toward him.

"Yes, well, it seemed to be the thing to do," Smoke said easily. "You were threatening that young lady, and throwing you off the train seemed to be the best way to take care of it."

"I'll bet you never expected to see Dingus Pugh again, did you?"

"That would be your name? Dingus Pugh?"

"That's the name, mister," Pugh said. He

smiled, a cold, evil smile. "I figured you might want to know the name of the man that's going to kill you. I see that you are wearing a gun. Get ready to use it."

At the challenge, those who were standing close to Smoke scattered quickly, moving to each end of the bar.

One person very pointedly did not move. Pearlie was standing next to Smoke, but he didn't even turn around to face Smoke's challenger. Instead, he leaned over the bar and called down to the bartender, who, like the others, had fled down to the far end of the bar.

"Mr. Barkeep, would you put a head on my beer, please?" Pearlie called.

"What?" the bartender answered in a nervous voice. "What do you want?"

Pearlie held up his beer mug. "I want you to refresh my beer, if you would. I've lost the head."

"You . . . you don't want me to do that right now, do you?"

"Well, I sure would appreciate it, if you don't mind," Pearlie said. "And what's wrong with right now?"

"Mister, are you blind, or just crazy?" the bartender asked. "There's a shoot-out about to take place, and you are right in the line of fire."

"Oh. Are you talking about that dumb turd standing in the door there? What did he say his name was? Dingus Pugh? Don't worry, I'm not in the line of fire. He won't even get a shot off. Smoke will put him down before he clears leather."

"Smoke?" the bartender said.

"Smoke Jensen," Pearlie said. "Now, about that beer, a cool one would be nice."

Smoke's name traveled all around the saloon, from mouth to mouth.

"Smoke."

"Smoke Jensen."

"I'll be damned. I've heard of 'im, never seen 'im before."

"You reckon that's really him?"

"Could be. Otherwise, why would he be standin' there so calm after someone's just said they're goin' to shoot him?"

"This'll be something to tell my grandkids. The day I seen Smoke Jensen kill somebody in a gunfight."

"Is that clock right? I want to remember the time this all happened."

When he heard Smoke Jensen's name, and the comments being made by the others in the saloon, beads of perspiration broke out on Dingus Pugh's forehead. His lower lip began to tremble, his mouth went dry, and he licked his lips nervously. His hand, which he was holding just over his pistol, began to shake visibly.

"Well, are you going to open the ball? Or just stand there with your thumb up your ass?" Smoke asked. His voice was as quiet and calm as if he were having a conversation over a cup of coffee.

Pugh stood there for a moment longer, neither speaking nor moving.

"Go away, Pugh," Smoke said. "I don't want to kill anyone today."

Pugh glared at Smoke, then put both hands up and shook his head. "No, sir," he said. "I ain't goin' to give you no excuse to kill me. No, sir."

Turning, he pushed back out through the swinging doors, chased by the laughter of everyone in the saloon.

Pugh stood just outside the saloon for a long moment, seething in rage. The anger he had felt over being thrown from the train was now compounded by the humiliation he had just experienced by being run out of the saloon.

That was when he saw the shotgun protruding from the saddle sheath of one of the horses tied to the hitching rail in front of the saloon. Grinning broadly, he grabbed the gun, a Winchester double-barrel twelve-gauge. Breaking it down, he checked the loads, then snapped it closed again. He stepped back up onto the porch.

Smoke just happened to glance in the mirror behind the bar when he saw Dingus Pugh charge back into the room, bent over, his shoulders thrust forward, his face set in a scowl. He was raising the shotgun to his shoulder even as he came in.

"You're going to die, you bastard!" he shouted loudly, pulling the trigger.

The gun roared and one of the barrels spewed flame.

Just before Pugh pulled the trigger, Smoke pushed Pearlie to one side while he dove to the floor on the other side. The shot passed so close overhead that he could feel the puff of air. Much of the heavy buckshot slammed into the top of the bar, ripping a big hole and sending out a shower of splinters. The rest of the load plowed into the shelf of bottles behind the bar, then into the mirror behind the bottle, bursting the mirror into several pieces of glass, from microscopic bits to large, dangling shards.

As the noise and smoke from the shotgun discharge filled the saloon, and before Pugh could fire the second barrel, Smoke Jensen returned fire. From his position on the floor, he was shooting up, and his bullet hit

Pugh just at the junction of his throat and chin. It penetrated the soft tissue, then burst from the back of his head, taking with it blood, brain matter, and chips of bone. It was all over before most people in the saloon had any idea that it was about to take place.

Chapter Nine

Within two hours after the shooting, an inquest was held before the Magistrate's Court, with Judge Spicer Wells presiding. Smoke had not been arrested, but he was asked to attend the inquest, and he did so without protest.

Nobody knew Dingus Pugh, and nobody would have even known the name had he not spoken it aloud when he came into the saloon. And though nearly everyone had heard of Smoke Jensen, only Bob Kleberg had ever met him, and Kleberg, who was not a witness to the shooting, had not been called. In fact, the inquest was already under way before Kleberg heard anything about it.

One by one the witnesses testified as to how Dingus Pugh had come into the saloon, challenging Smoke Jensen. They told how Jensen faced him down without drawing against him, and how Pugh left. Then they told how Pugh came running back into the room a second time, this time carrying Frank Clanton's shotgun.

"I don't know how he got the gun, Your Honor," Clanton answered when he was on the witness chair. "I was in the hardware store next door at the time and didn't even know what was goin' on till I heard the shootin'. Then, when I went into the saloon, why, I seen that it was my gun the feller on the floor was holdin'."

"And you did not give it to him?" Judge Wells asked.

"No, sir, I did not. And you can ask Cole Newton about that, seein' as he was waitin' on me in the store at the time."

"That's true, Judge," Newton said from the gallery. "Me'n Frank was talkin' about Muley Olsen's widder when we heard the shootin'."

Marie Olsen was a comely widow who, according to gossip, was being rather generous with her sexual charms. Newton's candid comment brought instantaneous laughter from the gallery, and Judge Wells had to bang his gavel several times to restore order.

"I'll have no more such outbursts in my court," he said. "And no talkin' 'less I call for it."

"All right, Your Honor, I won't talk no more," Newton said, and when Wells glared at him, the others in the courtroom laughed

136

again, though with considerably more restraint this time.

"Mr. Jensen, would you take the stand, please?"

"Yes, Your Honor," Smoke replied. Sally was sitting next to him in the court, and Pearlie and Cal were sitting next to Sally. Sally squeezed Smoke's hand as he stood up, then walked to the front of the courtroom. A Bible was thrust before him.

"Do you swear to tell the truth, the whole truth, and nothing but the truth, so help you God?"

"I do."

"Please take the witness chair."

"Now, your name is Smoke Jensen?" the judge asked.

"That's right."

"There is a man of some note, said to be very, very good with a gun, by the name of Smoke Jensen. In fact, I know that some dime novels have been written about Smoke Jensen. Are you that Smoke Jensen?"

"I am, Your Honor," Smoke said.

The judge smiled. "Well, Mr. Jensen, I don't know as I have ever met a genuine celebrity before. May I say that it is an honor and a privilege to meet you?"

"Thank you, Your Honor."

At that moment, Richard King and Bob Kleberg came into the courtroom. Henrietta and Alice were with them, and the four took their seats in the very last row. When Alice saw the man on the witness chair, she gasped.

"It's him!" she said.

Someone in the row just in front of her turned and glared, holding his finger across his lips in the sign to be quiet.

"Now, Mr. Jensen," the magistrate continued. "You have the reputation of being a brave and determined man, expert in the use of firearms, as quick as thought and as certain as death. I did not know Mr. Pugh, nor have we been able to find anyone who did know him. And since I have heard of you, but I have never heard of Dingus Pugh, is it not reasonable to assume that he was not as skilled with firearms as you are?"

Smoke nodded. "I suppose so, Your Honor, but I never take anyone for granted," he said. "However, I do try to avoid killing someone if I possibly can. And I tried to avoid this one as well."

"Yes, the witnesses do seem to support you in this. However, that does raise the question as to why he came after you in the first place. I believe witnesses have testified that he said you threw him off the train. Is that correct? Did you throw him off the train?"

"I did, Your Honor."

"Well, that in itself would seem motivation enough to drive a man to an intemperate action. Were you deliberately trying to provoke him?"

"No, Your Honor, he wasn't!" Alice said, standing up and speaking out loud to the surprise of everyone in the courtroom, including Kleberg and her parents. "He was protecting me."

Although Judge Wells had cautioned against speaking in court unless addressed, he recognized Alice King. He knew also that her father was not only the largest rancher in this part of Texas; he was also a very wealthy man who had heavily invested in several businesses in Corpus Christi. Taking all that into consideration, he did not chastise Alice for interrupting his court. Instead, he just followed up on her comment.

"Miss King, would you like to expand upon the statement you just made?"

"Do you want me to come up there and sit in the chair?" Alice said, pointing toward the witness chair.

"No, no, that won't be necessary," Judge Wells said. "You can stay where you are. The court reposes enough confidence in your veracity that you need not be sworn. But please tell us what you mean when you say Mr. Jensen was protecting you."

Alice told about seeing the man in the dining car while she was having her breakfast. She then told about trying to return to her car, only to be interrupted on the vestibule between cars.

"He took out his gun, covered it with his hat, and pointed it at me. That was when Mr. Jensen happened to pass by. At first, I thought he didn't realize I was in danger, because he just went on. Then, a moment later, he reappeared from the car, grabbed the man who was accosting me, and threw him from the train."

"Hear, hear!" someone shouted out loud, and the rest of the courtroom gallery cheered and applauded.

"Order!" Judge Wells said, slamming his gavel against his desktop. "Order!"

Finally, the court was quiet.

"Mr. Jensen, I will accept the young lady's testimony as to your motivation. However, I cannot but wonder if there would not have been a better way for you to deal with him upon the occurrence of your first meeting than the injudicious act of throwing him from the train.

"On the other hand, when we consider

140

the condition of affairs incidental to a frontier country, the lawlessness and disregard for human life, the existence of a law-defying element in our midst, the fear and feeling of insecurity that has existed, the supposed prevalence of bad, desperate, and reckless men who have been a terror to the country and kept away capital and enterprise, and considering the testimony of those who witnessed the event of this morning, I can attach no criminality to your act. I am therefore going to find that the decedent, Dingus Pugh, died by an act of justifiable homicide." Again, the judge banged his gavel. "This court is adjourned."

With the adjournment of the court, nearly everyone rushed to Smoke to shake his hand in congratulations, though for many, it was merely an excuse to meet the legendary Smoke Jensen.

Alice, her parents, and Bob Kleberg hung back for a long time, waiting until nearly everyone else was gone before they approached him.

"I didn't get a chance to thank you before," Alice said.

Smoke smiled. "You thanked me enough a few minutes ago when you convinced the judge that I didn't toss that fella off the train just for the fun of it."

"Smoke," Kleberg said, stepping forward then. "This is Captain Richard King, my employer, and the owner —"

"Of the Santa Gertrudis Ranch," Smoke said, finishing the sentence. "I'm a rancher as well," he said, extending his hand to shake the hand of Richard King. "I don't believe there is a rancher in the country who hasn't heard of Captain King, the ranch, and the Santa Gertrudis breed of cattle. It's an honor to meet you."

"The honor is all mine," King said. "And you have my gratitude, sir, for coming to the aid of my daughter in her time of danger."

"Anyone would have done it," Smoke said. "Oh, let me introduce you to my wife and friends."

Smoke introduced Sally, Pearlie, and Cal; then he met Henrietta.

"Captain King is the reason I asked you to come down," Kleberg said after all the introductions were completed.

"Oh?"

"Yes," King said. "And I want to apologize, Mr. Jensen, for doubting you. That is, doubting the type of person you are. You see, I did not want to resort to using a gunfighter to fight my battle for me. I thought . . . well, never mind what I thought. I was wrong. And if you are still willing to offer your assistance, I would be more than willing to accept it. In fact, I'll go beyond that. I'm asking for your assistance."

"I came down to do whatever I could do to help my old friend Bob Kleberg," Smoke said. "And since that means helping you, I will be glad to do anything I can for you."

"Wonderful!" King said, smiling broadly. "Uh, where are you staying now?"

"We've taken rooms in the Dunn Hotel."

"We're there as well," King said. "We were going to start back today, but . . ."

"There's a dance there tonight," Alice said, interrupting her father.

"And she wants to go for some reason," King teased. He looked directly at Kleberg. "Though, for the life of me, I don't know why."

Kleberg cleared his throat in embarrassment.

"At any rate, if you are still willing to help me, despite my bad-mannered rejection of your earlier offer, I would like for all of you to come back to the ranch with us tomorrow."

"There's no need for you to put yourself out on our account," Smoke said. "We can stay here . . . or take accommodations somewhere closer to the ranch."

"Nonsense. There is nothing closer to the

ranch than Corpus Christi, certainly nothing that would be a decent place for you to stay. You'll be my guests at the ranch, and I won't take no for an answer. Besides, you'll be much more comfortable, and I know you will eat better."

"Eat?" Pearlie said, breaking into a large smile.

Smoke chuckled. "You've just said the magic word for my friend."

"Your friend likes to eat, does he?" King asked.

"He will eat anything that doesn't eat him first," Smoke said.

"And if it plans to eat him first, it better get a head start," Cal said.

The others laughed at Cal's observation.

There was one person in the court who had not joined the others when they gathered around Smoke Jensen; nor had he left the moment court was adjourned. But while he hung around for a while longer, just to see what connection there was between Smoke Jensen and Captain King, Brad Preston stayed in the back of the court in order to make certain Smoke didn't see him. He knew that probably wasn't necessary. His encounter with Jensen had been so brief, and so long ago, that he was sure Jensen wouldn't remember it now.

Earlier in the day, when both Manning and Waco Jones drank themselves into insensibility, the owner of the Gold Strike Saloon had the two men dragged out into the alley to sleep it off. Preston, who had drunk much less, left the Gold Strike and continued exploring the town. That was when he heard of the inquest into the shooting that had taken place a couple of hours earlier.

"Who did you say got hisself killed?" Preston asked.

"They say his name was Dingus Pugh, but don't nobody seem to know him," he was answered. "Why? Did you know him? 'Cause if you did, they got him on show in the front window down at Wagner's hardware store."

"No," Preston lied, shaking his head. "I've never heard of him."

Drawn by honest curiosity, as well as morbid interest, Preston walked down to look through the hardware-store window. There, in a plain pine coffin, tipped up for better viewing, was the body of Dingus Pugh. He was wearing a jacket that was too small as well as a stiff collar and tie. His arms were folded across his chest, and he was holding a white lily.

Preston had seen such displays before. He

knew that the clothes belonged to the undertaker and were just for showing. He knew also that, before the pine box was closed, the clothes would be removed.

There was a sign in the window.

DO YOU KNOW THIS MAN?

As Preston stood there staring at the body, he felt a chill pass over him. He knew that this could very easily be his body lying there in a pine box. Once, ten years ago, he had drawn his gun against Jensen, but before he could even get his gun out, Jensen had hit him on the head, knocking him out.

Now, the son of a bitch was here, had shot Pugh, and was receiving accolades from those who attended the inquest.

As Preston listened in on the conversation, he learned that Smoke Jensen intended to help Richard King. And if that was the case, this was information that Major Brandt would need to know.

Once again, Preston checked in on Manning and Waco Jones, intending to tell them that they needed to get back to Concepcion, but they were both still passed out in the alley behind the Gold Strike.

"Manning, Waco, get up," he said, kicking on the sole of Manning's boot.

"Manning, wake up!" He kicked again.

Manning growled, and turned over. "Go away," he said.

"Waco. Get up," Preston said. "We've got to go back now."

"I want another drink," Waco mumbled.

Sighing, Preston stared down at them for a moment longer, then shrugged.

"You two are worthless as tits on a boar hog," he said.

He didn't have time to wait on them. This was news he had to get back to Major Brandt right away. Preston went back into the saloon, and when the bartender came over to him, he bought a beer to drink before he started his long ride back.

"Bartender, do me a favor," Preston said. He nodded toward the back. "When my two friends wake up, tell them I went back."

The bartender didn't answer, but he nodded affirmatively as he wiped the bar off with a towel.

As Preston rode out of town, he passed a big sign spread across the road that read:

CATTLEMEN'S DANCE TONIGHT
ALL WELCOME

Chapter Ten

Since Captain King and the others would not be starting back to the ranch until the following day, all decided to attend the dance that night. By dusk, the excitement that had been growing for the entire day was full-blown. The sound of the practicing musicians could be heard all up and down Shoreline Street. Children gathered around the glowing, yellow windows on the ground floor of the hotel and peered inside. The ballroom floor was cleared of all tables and chairs, and the musicians had been installed on the platform at the front of the room.

The band started with several numbers — "Buffalo Gals," "The Gandy Dancers' Ball," and "Little Joe the Wrangler" being the most popular. Horses and buckboards began arriving, and soon every hitching rail on Shoreline Street, and even up Star Street all the way to Mesquite Street, was full. Men and women streamed along the boardwalks toward the hotel, the women in colorful ginghams, the men in clean, blue denims and brightly decorated vests.

Cal and Pearlie were in their room on the third floor of the hotel, getting ready to go downstairs to the dance. Actually, Cal was ready, and he was standing at the open window, looking down at those who were arriving. From there, he could hear the high skirling of the fiddle. Behind him, Pearlie was still shaving.

"Will you hurry up?" Cal asked. "By the time you get finished primping, the dance will be over."

"Just because you are too young to shave doesn't mean I don't have to," Pearlie said as he wiped off the last of the lather.

"Ha! I have to shave."

"Yes, but with you, it's not an art yet," Pearlie said. He started to reach for his gun belt.

"You aren't going to take your gun, are you?"

Pearlie snickered. "No, I reckon not," he said. "I'm not likely to need a gun at a dance now, am I?"

Leaving their room, they knocked on the door to Smoke's room.

"Smoke," Pearlie called. "You and Miss Sally comin', or what?"

"We'll be there," Smoke's muffled voice replied from inside. "Go on down."

"Let's go," Pearlie said.

"If you're waitin' on me, you're backin' up," Cal said as he started clomping down the stairs.

Pearlie joined him and when the two reached the ground floor, they hurried toward the sound of the music and laughter.

Once they were inside, the excitement was all it promised to be. Several young women were gathered on one side of the room, giggling and turning their heads in embarrassment as young men, just as embarrassed, made awkward attempts to flirt with them. At the back of the dance floor there was a large punch bowl on a table and Cal saw one of the cowboys look around to make certain he wasn't being seen, then pour whiskey into the punch bowl from a bottle he had concealed beneath his vest. A moment later, another cowboy did the same thing, and Cal laughed.

"What is it?" Pearlie asked.

"Nothin'," Cal replied. "I think I'll just get me some punch."

Pearlie watched Cal walk around the edge of the dance floor to the punch bowl, then looked toward the area where the men and women who were with each other were waiting. Bob Kleberg and Alice King, who

150

had come down before them, were with this group. Alice waved at Pearlie as he stood watching.

Cal came back with two cups of punch and handed one to Pearlie, just as Smoke and Sally arrived. Sally reached for Cal's cup and smelled it, then poured it out into a potted plant.

"Aw, Miss Sally," Cal protested.

"Not until you are a little older," Sally insisted.

"Choose up your squares!" the caller shouted through his megaphone, and several couples, including Smoke and Sally and Kleberg and Alice, hurried to their positions within one of the squares. Pearlie and Cal joined the cowboys who were advancing toward the unattached girls, and when a couple of pretty red-haired girls accepted their invitation to dance, they made up the final two sets for the square that had Smoke and Sally and Bob and Alice.

The music began then, with the fiddles loud and clear, the guitars carrying the rhythm, the accordion providing the counterpoint, and the Dobro singing over everything. The caller began to shout, and he clapped his hands and stomped his feet and danced around on the platform in compliance with his own calls, bowing and whirling as if he had a girl and was in one of the squares himself. The dancers moved and swirled to the caller's commands.

"Swing your partner round and round,
Turn your corner upside down.
Hang on tight like swingin' on a gate,
Meet your partner for a grand chain eight,
Chew some 'backy and dip some snuff,
Grab your honey and strut your stuff."

Around the dance floor sat those who were without partners, looking on wistfully, those who were too old holding back those who were too young. At the punch bowl table, cowboys continued to add their own ingredients, and though many drank from the punch bowl, the contents of the bowl never seemed to diminish.

Two men lay behind the Gold Strike Saloon. That they were lying in the offal and refuse of the saloon, including the place where the spittoons were emptied, didn't seem to matter to them. A dog cocked his leg and peed on Manning's face.

Manning wiped at his face, then blinked his eyes a couple of times. Looking around, he saw that it was dark and that he was lying on the ground behind a building. Waco was with him. He sat up, then reached over to nudge Waco's shoulder.

"Hey," Manning said. "Waco."

Waco didn't respond, and Manning nudged him again. "Waco, you alive or dead?"

"Hrmmph," Waco grunted.

"Get up," Manning said.

Waco sat up and smacked his lips a few times, looking around him.

"Damn, I feel like shit," Waco said.

"No wonder. We're lyin' out here in the alley like some damn drunk or somethin'," Manning said.

"Where the hell are we?" Waco asked.

"I don't know exactly. But if I was to guess, I'd say we're out in the alley behind some saloon."

"Which saloon?"

"The one we was drinkin' in, I guess."

"Where's Preston?"

"I don't know. I ain't seen him since he went to the depot to meet that fella we were here to meet."

"You mean Pugh?" Waco asked.

"Yeah, Pugh. Dingus Pugh."

"Wonder if he got 'im."

"Prob'ly," Manning said. "What I'm wonderin' is if maybe Preston ain't the son of a bitch put us out here."

Groaning, Manning stood up and looked around for his hat, then finding it, put it on. "Come on, get up," he said. "Unless you want to spend the night out here. You're actin' like you ain't never been passed out drunk before."

"Don't know as I have," Waco replied. "Leastwise, I ain't never been passed out in no alley before."

Waco got to his feet. He had been lying in the residue of several emptied spittoons, and he spent a moment brushing bits and pieces of tobacco from his clothes. He was unable to do anything about the brown stains.

"What do we do now?" Waco asked.

"I don't know. Try and find Preston and Pugh, I reckon. But I don't have an idea in hell as to where to start."

Manning and Waco Jones went back into the Gold Strike Saloon. They were surprised to see so few people inside. When they stepped up to the bar, the bartender slid down toward them.

"I see you fellas got sobered up. Back for another go-around, are you?"

"Yeah," Waco said. "Hey, how'd we wind up sleepin' in the alley anyhow?"

"I had you carried out there," the bartender said.

"You are the one who done that?" Waco asked angrily.

"Yes, but you don't need to thank me," the bartender answered. "I mean, you was both passed out on the table. I figured you'd be more comfortable layin' down than all slumped over like that. You was, wasn't you?"

"Was what?" Waco asked, confused by the fact that, instead of being defensive about it, the bartender was taking pride in telling about it.

"You was more comfortable layin' down than slumped over the table," he said. "Leastwise, you looked like you was. I checked on you a couple of times just to make sure you was all right. You was both sleepin' like babies."

"Uh, yeah," Waco said, his anger defused. "Yeah, I guess we was more comfortable."

"Lots of barkeeps would just leave you at the table, but not me. No, sir. For me, it's a matter of pride that I take care of my customers as best I can. And I don't expect no tip nor nothin' neither."

"Well, that's good, 'cause you ain't goin' to get no tip from us," Manning said.

"That's all right. Like I said, I ain't expectin' one. So, what can I do for you gents now that you have rejoined the land of the living?"

"Whiskey," Waco said.

"Same," Manning added.

The bartender pulled the cork on a bottle and filled two glasses.

"What happened to them other two fingers?" the bartender asked, looking at the three fingers on Manning's left hand.

"They got bit off in a fight," Manning said.

"Damn."

Manning chuckled. "That's okay. I bit off his ear."

"It's a wonder you didn't kill each other."

"He was my brother or I would'a killed the sum bitch," Manning said.

The two men took their glasses, then turned their backs to the bar and looked out over the nearly empty room. There were no bar girls working the place and nobody was playing the piano. There were only four customers in the saloon, one standing alone at the far end of the bar and three more sitting at a table.

"Oh," the bartender said. "Your friend told me to tell you that he was going to go on back without you."

"Our friend? You mean Preston?"

"Didn't give me his name. He just asked

me to tell you that he was goin' on back without you, which is what I just done."

"Both of 'em?" Manning asked.

"Both of 'em?" the bartender replied. He shook his head. "There was only one that I saw."

"I thought Preston come to pick up . . . what was that fella's name again?" Waco asked.

"Pugh," Manning replied. "Dingus Pugh."

"Yeah, Dingus Pugh. Well, maybe he didn't make the train and that's why Preston went on back."

"What was that name you just said?" the bartender asked. "Did you say Dingus Pugh?"

"Yeah. We was supposed to meet him here. If he made the train, that is."

"Oh, he made the train, all right," the bartender said.

"You've seen him then?"

"I've seen 'im," the bartender answered. "You can too, if you walk down the street and look in through the window down to the hardware store."

"What are you talkin' about?"

"If you two boys hadn't been passed out drunk in the alley all day, you would know that a fella by the name of Dingus Pugh got hisself shot," the customer standing at the end of the bar said, joining the conversation then. "He's laid out in the front window of the hardware store, all dressed up as pretty as you please."

"The hell you say."

"Go down there and check it out, if you don't believe me."

"Son of a bitch," Waco said. "I wonder if Preston shot him."

"Nope," the talkative customer said. "He was shot by a fella name of Jensen. Smoke Jensen."

"Smoke Jensen, you say?" Waco asked, perking up at the mention of the name.

"Yep."

"Who is Smoke Jensen?" Manning asked. "I've never heard of him."

"Then you're a fool," Waco said.

"Say what?"

"Smoke Jensen is just about the most famous gunfighter there is," Waco said. Almost without any awareness of what he was doing, Waco loosened the pistol in his holster. "But there ain't never been a man that couldn't be beat, and someday, somebody's goin' to put him down. I'll say this. Whoever kills Smoke Jensen is goin' to get hisself quite a name."

"Ha," the man at the end of the bar said. "Well, it sure as hell ain't goin' to be you, sonny."

Waco's face grew cold, and he turned to face the man at the end of the bar.

"Mister, you ain't sayin' that I'm not fast enough, are you?" Waco asked.

Realizing that he might have overstepped himself, the man at the end of the bar turned toward Waco. He cleared his throat, nervously.

"I . . . I'm not sayin' nothin' of the sort," he said. "I don't know you. I don't know how fast you are."

"Why don't you find out?" Waco asked.

"What?"

"Why don't you find out if I'm fast enough?"

"Look, mister, I got no quarrel with you."

"Yeah, you do," Waco said. "You just picked one with me."

"Waco, why don't you let it be?" Manning said.

"Huh-uh," Waco replied. "He started it. Now I aim to finish it."

"Mister, please," the man standing at the bar said. "I didn't mean nothin' by what I said."

"Oh? Then you think I can beat Smoke Jensen?"

"I . . . I don't know. I've never seen either one of you draw."

"Well, now is your chance."

"No! Please! Mister, I've got a wife and kids. The bartender will tell you I didn't mean nothin' by it. Eddie, tell 'im!" the man pleaded. "For God's sake, tell 'im I ain't no gunfighter."

"I know Willie," the bartender said. "He works for a freight company, and he's a good man. I know he didn't mean no insult."

"So, I'm just supposed to let him off scot-free, am I?" Waco asked. "I mean, after he challenged me like he done?"

"I didn't challenge you," Willie said, his voice hanging on the edge of panic.

"Oh, so now you are calling me a liar," Waco said. "I don't like it when someone calls me a liar." He pulled his pistol slowly and deliberately.

The expression on Willie's face was one of desperation. It seemed that everything he said just made it worse.

"Oh, my God! My God! Please, mister, please," Willie begged, now shaking visibly. "Please don't shoot me. I didn't mean nothin' by it, I swear I didn't!" Willie covered his eyes with his hands.

Waco cocked his pistol and aimed it at Willie.

"Jesus, Waco, what are you doing?" Manning asked. "Killin' him ain't worth you goin' to jail over."

The front of Willie's pants grew wet and, seeing it, Waco laughed and lowered his pistol.

"Well, now, lookie there," Waco said. "It looks like you had yourself a little accident there, Willie boy. Go home and tell your wife and kids that I made you pee in your pants."

"Yes, sir," Willie mumbled. "Yes, sir. Thank you for not killing me."

Waco laughed hysterically as Willie hurried out of the saloon. Then he turned toward the bartender. "I wasn't really goin' to kill him," he said. "I was just havin' a little fun with him."

The bartender, having seen a side of Waco that he didn't want to cross, laughed nervously. "It was funny all right, seeing Willie wet himself like that."

Waco looked around the saloon. "Damn, there wasn't hardly nobody here to see the show. Where the hell is everyone?" he asked.

"They're all at the dance."

"What dance?"

"Ever' month, 'specially during the summer, the cattlemen hold a dance down at the Dunn Hotel," the bartender answered. "It's supposed to be for the good of the town but if you ask me, it ain't all that good for the saloons. Hell, everyone winds

161

up down there and there don't nobody does come into any of the saloons. I think it's bad for business."

"A dance, huh?" Manning said as he tossed his whiskey down. "Hey, Waco, what do you say we go down to that there dance the barkeep is talkin' about?"

"What for?"

"Damn, Waco, use your head," Manning said. "If there's dancin' down there, there's bound to be women. Wouldn't you like to be around some women for a change? Other'n Becky, I mean?"

Waco smiled. "Yeah, you're right. Okay, let's go get us a couple of women," he said.

"Wait," Manning said.

"What?"

"We need to spiff up a bit. I mean, we're kind of dirty and stinky to be around women."

Waco held his arm up and sniffed it. "Oh, I don't know as we smell all that bad."

Manning laughed. "Believe me, you smell bad."

"I don't smell no worse than you do."

"We both smell bad. You got another shirt in your saddlebag?"

"Yeah, but it's the one I'd been wearin' before I put on this here clean one to come into town in."

"Put it back on," Manning said. "It's cleaner'n the one you're wearin'. We can wash up in the horse trough."

The two men left and Eddie, the bartender, walked over to look out, to make certain they were gone.

"Damn," Eddie said. "I'd hate to see the woman who would take up with the likes of them two."

The three remaining customers in the bar laughed, but they didn't laugh very loud. They had seen enough of Waco.

Chapter Eleven

At the Dunn Hotel, the caller called his last call, the fiddler played his last few bars, and the music stopped. Laughing, the dancers left the floor with Pearlie and Cal escorting the two redheaded girls back to the area where they'd met them.

"I'm Sue and this is Jane," one of the girls said to Pearlie. "We're sisters. Are you two brothers?"

Pearlie looked at Cal and realized that he was probably the closest thing to a brother he had. Smiling, he nodded. "Yeah," he said. "I don't like to claim him, but he's my brother."

"Isn't this wonderful?" Jane said. "We're sisters, you are brothers, and here we are together."

"Would you like some punch?" Cal asked.

Sue made a face and shook her head. "No. Have you tasted that punch? It is awful."

"Oh," Cal said, obviously disappointed that yet another attempt to drink the punch had been thwarted.

"I don't believe I've seen you two before,"

Sue said. "Do you work at one of the ranches?"

"We ride for the Sugarloaf," Cal said proudly.

The two girls looked at each other in confusion. "The Sugarloaf?" Jane said. "I don't think I know it."

"Well, it's just about the finest ranch there is, is all," Cal said.

"The reason you haven't heard of it is because it is up in Colorado," Pearlie said. "Sometimes my . . . brother . . . forgets some of the details."

"Oh, yeah," Cal said. "Maybe I did forget to say that."

"So, you have come all the way down here from Colorado? How fascinating!" Jane said, batting long eyelashes at Cal.

Cal pulled at his collar in embarrassment. "Uh, yeah," he said. "It's, uh, fascinating all right."

"Form your squares!" the caller shouted.

"Oh . . . another dance!" Sue said, looking pointedly at Pearlie.

"Shall we go again?" Pearlie asked, holding out his arm.

"I'd be delighted," Sue replied.

Jane didn't even wait to be asked. She just took Cal's arm, and Cal smiled broadly as they returned to the floor for another dance.

★ ★ ★

When Manning and Waco stepped into the hotel ballroom, a dance was already in progress and out on the floor couples moved and skipped, swayed and bowed as the music played and the caller called. In addition to the dancers, there were several unattached men standing around the sides of the room, watching.

"Looks like there's a lot more men than women," Manning said. He nodded at a group of women standing together. "There's some women over there that ain't dancin'."

Waco looked toward the women. "Damn," he said. "No wonder they ain't dancin'. They're uglier than a stump." He looked around the room. "I'm thirsty. Ain't there no bar in this place?"

"There's a punch bowl over there," Manning said.

"Punch? You mean like fruit juice and shit? Hell, I don't want punch. I want somethin' to drink."

Manning chuckled. "You ain't been to many things like this, have you?"

"I ain't never been to nothin' like this," Waco admitted.

"Nothin'? You mean ain't never been to a weddin' or a wake, or nothin' like that?"

"No."

166

"Well, believe me, at things like this, punch ain't what you think it is. Come on."

The two men walked over to the table to get a cup of punch. Because they were so dirty and odorous, people moved away from them like Moses parting the water.

Neither Manning nor Waco noticed the reaction they were getting, or if they did notice, they paid no attention. Waco got a glass of punch, then smiled after he took the first swallow. "You're right. This here ain't half bad," he said.

The set ended and the couples left the floor. Waco finished his drink, then wiped his hand across his mouth.

"What do you say we go get us a couple of good-lookin' women?" he suggested.

"You got someone in mind?"

"Yeah," Waco said, pointing. "How 'bout them two redheaded ones over there?"

"Can you really see snow on top of the mountains?" Jane asked.

"Sure can," Cal replied. "All year long."

"Oh, I would love to see such a thing. I've never seen mountains so high. I've never even seen snow. It must be beautiful."

"I reckon it's pretty if you're lookin' at it from a long ways off. But if you're standing hip-deep in it, and trying to mend a fence to keep the wolves away from your cows, well, it can get downright miserable," Cal said. He shivered. "And I've done that a lot of times," he added.

"Oh, I think that would be very exciting," Jane said, again flirting with him.

"Hey, you two good-lookin' women," someone said. "My name's Waco, and this here fella is called Manning. What are your names?"

Cal looked over at the speaker. There were two men standing there, one about his age, the other a little older. He noticed that the older one was missing two fingers on his left hand. Although Cal was irritated by the intrusion, he knew that neither he nor Pearlie had any claim on Sue and Jane. It was up to them to respond in whatever way they wanted.

Neither Sue nor Jane made any response at all.

"How about leavin' them dumb-lookin' galoots 'n comin' with us?"

This time Jane very pointedly turned her back on Waco.

"Hey, don't you turn your back on me when I talkin' to you!" Waco said angrily. He reached to grab Jane by her shoulder and jerked her around roughly.

Reacting almost before he thought, Cal

swung his fist, catching Waco on the point of his chin, knocking him down.

By now the fracas had caught everyone's attention, and all looked over to see what was going on.

"Sorry about knockin' you down like that, mister," Cal said, stepping forward to offer his hand to help Waco back on his feet. "But that wasn't very polite of you to grab the young lady like that."

Scowling at Cal, Waco let him help him back to his feet. Then the scowl turned to an evil smile as he stared at Cal with his hand hanging loosely over his pistol.

"Draw, mister," Waco said.

"Well, now, that's going to be pretty hard to do, isn't it?" Cal said. "I'm not wearing a gun."

"Get yourself one," Waco said. "Get one from your dumb-looking friend there." He nodded toward Pearlie.

"I'm not carrying a gun either," Pearlie said.

"What kind of coward doesn't carry a gun?"

"This is a hotel ballroom, not a saloon. Gentlemen don't come to places like this carrying a pistol," another voice said.

Turning, Waco saw a man who was somewhat older than the two he was accosting.

"You'd do well to stay out of this, mister. You don't have a stake in this."

"Yes, I do. You see, those two men happen to be friends of mine."

"Who the hell are you?"

"The name is Kirby."

"Kirby, is it? Well, who invited you into this, *Kirby?*" Waco came down hard on the name Kirby, obviously amused by it.

"You might say I invited myself." Moving his jacket to one side, he disclosed the fact that he was wearing a pistol.

"Ha!" Waco said. "I thought you said gentlemen don't come to a place like this wearing a gun."

"Well, see, that's the problem," Smoke said with an easy grin. "I guess I'm not quite the gentleman I should be. I'm sure my wife would like me to be a bit more gentlemanly at times. Right, Sally?"

"Right, Smoke," Sally said. "Though even I will admit that this doesn't seem to be one of those times. When you are dealing with riffraff like this, you can be as unruly as you want."

"Smoke?" Waco asked. "Did she call you Smoke?" His face registered his confusion.

"Yes. Well, maybe I should explain. My name really is Kirby. Kirby Jensen. But most folks, my wife included, call me Smoke."

"You're Smoke Jensen?"

Smoke nodded, but he didn't answer.

Waco licked his lips, then glanced over toward Manning. Manning was watching with interest, but it was very obvious that he was not going to take a hand in whatever was about to happen.

"Look," Waco said, pointing to Smoke. "I told you. This here ain't between us. This here is between me and this fella."

Smoke shook his head slowly. "But as you can see, I've sort of stepped in here to make it my business," Smoke said. "So, what's your next move? Do you draw on me? Or do you take your stinking carcass out of here so decent people can continue to have a good time?"

Waco stood there for a long moment, trying to build up the courage to take the next step. Smoke followed the struggle in Waco's eyes, saw when he almost reached the courage it would take to pull his gun. And he saw too when Waco lost whatever nerve he had built up. The anger, defiance, and courage drained away.

"Like I . . . uh . . . told you, this here ain't your fight," Waco said. Then, mustering as much defiance and maintaining as much dignity as he could, he turned to his friend.

"Come on, Manning. Let's get out of

here," Waco said. "There ain't nothin' here but a bunch of cowards and fluffed-up dandies."

The others at the dance watched in stunned silence as Waco and Manning left the ballroom of the hotel. A few, though not all of them, realized that they had just avoided seeing a deadly confrontation.

"Let's get the music goin'!" the caller shouted and, once again, the band began playing.

"That's the bravest thing I've ever seen," Jane said, taking Cal's arm in both her hands. She looked up at him with large, blue eyes that could melt butter.

"Smoke is pretty brave all right," Cal said.

"No, silly, I'm not talking about Mr. Jensen," Jane said. "I'm talking about you. You defended my honor, even though he was armed and you weren't."

"Yeah," Pearlie agreed, smiling at his younger friend. "You did me proud."

Cal beamed as he escorted Jane out onto the floor for the next dance.

Smoke and Sally stayed out of this one because the sheriff came over to talk to Smoke.

"Do you know that man?" the sheriff asked.

"No," Smoke replied. "Should I?"

"Probably not. His name is Waco Jones.

He's very fast with a gun, and has killed at least seven men that I know of."

"Why isn't he in jail?"

"So far, every killing has been ruled as justifiable homicide," the sheriff said. "Though on at least half of them, they say he goaded the other man into drawing first. Word is, he is trying to build a reputation."

Smoke nodded. "I've run across his kind before, and I'm sure I'll run across his kind again."

"Be careful, Mr. Jensen," the sheriff said. "I have a gut feeling about these things, and I'm pretty sure you'll run across him again."

"You think he wants to put my notch on his gun handle, do you?" Smoke asked.

The sheriff nodded. "I'd bet on it," he said.

"Yeah. Well, I wouldn't take you up on the bet," Smoke said. "I think you might be right."

"Smoke," Sally said as the sheriff walked away.

"I know," Smoke said. "You don't have to tell me."

"But I'm going to tell you anyway," Sally said. "Please be careful."

Just out of town, Three-Finger Manning and Waco Jones were riding through the night, their way lighted by a very bright, full moon.

Manning chuckled.

"What is it you are a'laughin' at?"

"I ain't laughin' at nothing," Manning said.

They rode on for a few moments longer, the silence broken only by the clopping of their horses' hooves. Manning chuckled again.

"I asked you what it was you was a'laughin' at," Waco demanded, more angrily this time.

"I thought you was goin' to show ever'one how you was faster than Smoke Jensen."

"I *am* faster!" Waco insisted.

"Uh-huh," Manning said sarcastically. "I seen how much faster you was." He laughed again.

"Tonight wasn't the right time or place, is all," Waco said.

"I'm sure it wasn't."

"I couldn't of kilt him in there with all those witnesses. I mean, even if it had been a fair fight, you know half the folks there would say I drew first."

"You're probably right." Manning chuckled again. "Course the thing is, if you had drawed down on him, you wouldn't be needin' to worry none about what any of the witnesses would'a said 'cause you'd be dead."

Waco spurred his horse so that it leaped forward several feet; then he spun it around so he was facing Manning.

"All right, if you think I'm slow, maybe you'd like to try me. Unless you are afraid of me."

"Oh, I'm not afraid of you," Manning said.

"You ought to be."

"I don't think so. If anyone should be scared, it should be you."

"Me? Scared of you? Now, why should I be scared of you?"

There was a metallic clicking sound in the night.

"What was that?" Waco asked.

Manning pulled his poncho to one side, revealing the fact that he was holding a double-barreled shotgun leveled toward Waco. "That clicking sound you heard was the reason you should be scared of me," Manning said. "I'm fixin' to blow your ass to hell and back."

Manning raised the shotgun to his shoulder.

"No, hold it!" Waco shouted, holding his hands out in front of him. "Manning, wait! Look, I didn't mean nothin' by all that talk of drawin' against you." Waco forced a weak laugh. "Can't you take a joke? I was just funnin' with you, is all."

"I don't like jokes, and I'm not funning," Manning said, continuing to hold the shotgun on Waco, the twin barrels unwavering.

"Manning, please," Waco said in a voice that, for the first time, showed Manning just how young Waco really was.

Sighing, Manning lowered the gun. "Look, kid, I'm a lot older'n you are," he said. "And I've run across a lot of fast guns in my day, most all of 'em faster'n me. But I'm still alive. Do you want to know the reason I'm still alive?"

Waco nodded.

"The reason I'm still alive is I don't play games. If I think someone is a threat to me, I kill 'em. I don't face them in a fair fight 'cause I don't care about getting myself some kind of a reputation. All I care about is staying alive, do you understand that?"

"Yes," Waco replied, his voice still young and thin.

"Good, I'm glad you do. Because I'm tellin' you right here and right now, if you plan to keep on playing this game with me, then I'm going to shoot you, and I guarantee you, I will kill you."

"You don't want to do that," Waco said. "I mean, it's like Major Brandt said, we're all on the same side."

"Then no more talk about how fast you are," Manning said. "Otherwise, whether you're sleepin', eatin', or shittin', you're goin' to have to be lookin' over your shoulder. Do you get my meanin'?"

"Yeah," Waco said. "Now, put the scattergun away."

"Thank you, but I'll just keep it handy for the rest of our ride back."

Chapter Twelve

When Richard King started back home on the following day, his entourage drew quite a bit of attention. He, Kleberg, Smoke, Cal, and Pearlie were on horseback. Henrietta, Alice, and Sally were in a Concord coach. In sturdiness and construction, it was the same kind used on the commercial stagecoach lines, though this one had been built with deep-cushioned leather seats and tapestry on the floors and walls. The doors of the coach had glass windows that could be rolled up or down. The exterior glistened with several coats of burgundy lacquer. King's personal brand, the "running W," was gold-embossed on either door. Pulled by six horses, the coach had a driver and an armed guard.

Sally's horse was tied on behind the coach.

Three wagons, carrying luggage and purchases, followed the coach. Two men were in each wagon, and four more rode on horses behind the wagons. The entourage stretched out for a city block.

The editor of the newspaper took a photo of them just before they left, then hurried back to develop it so he could have a woodcut artist reproduce the photograph so that he could run the picture in a future issue.

Sue and Jane came down to see them off and Pearlie and Cal, seeing the two girls in the crowd, rode over to speak with them.

"We certainly had a nice time dancing with you two boys," Jane said.

"Will you be coming back for the dance next month?" Sue asked.

"I don't know," Pearlie answered. "More'n likely, we won't be back. But we had a good time too, didn't we, Cal?"

"We sure did," Cal said. He looked directly at Jane. "I think you're about the prettiest girl I ever danced with."

"Oh, my," Jane said, turning her head in embarrassment. "I'm sure that isn't the case, but it is certainly sweet of you to say so."

"All right!" King shouted then, standing in his stirrups and looking back along the train. "Let's head 'em out!"

The drivers whistled and snapped their whips then, and the train started out with a clopping of hooves and the rolling of wheels. Children and dogs ran down the street alongside them for a short distance, the children laughing and shouting and the dogs barking. Finally they reached the edge of town, then started west along Rogers Road.

As they rode along the road, bound for the Santa Gertrudis Ranch, King pointed out all the points of interest. Meanwhile, back in the coach, Sally painted a smile on her face and listened to the conversation and gossip of Henrietta and her daughter. From time to time Sally would gaze wistfully through the window to catch a view of Smoke, or Pearlie, or one of the others on horseback, and wish that she could just say good-bye to the ladies in the coach and join them.

When they reached the little town of San Diego, they left the public road, and started south on a road that was built, owned, and maintained by the Santa Gertrudis Ranch.

"Where have you two been?" Brandt asked when Manning and Waco walked into the Gato Rojo Saloon in Concepcion the next day.

"We was in Corpus Christi with Preston," Manning said. "Listen, your man Pugh got hisself kilt. I don't know where Preston got off to but . . ." Manning stopped in mid-sentence when he saw Preston leaning back against the bar, watching him. "What the hell are you doing here?" he asked.

"You two was passed out drunk, Pugh was dead, and I didn't see no need in hanging around any longer," Preston answered.

"Yeah, well, maybe if you had stayed longer you would know who kilt Pugh," Waco said. He turned to Brandt. "It was —"

"Smoke Jensen," Brandt said, interrupting him.

"Oh."

"That's why I came back early," Preston said. "I figured Major Brandt needed to know about Jensen."

"Well, I figured he might be interested, but I don't know as he needs to know," Manning said.

"You don't think he would need to know that Jensen has come down here to help King?"

Manning looked shocked. "Smoke Jensen has come down to ride for Richard King?"

"Yes."

"I don't believe it. Why would he do something like that? You must be wrong."

"I heard it with my own ears," Preston said.

"Good," Waco said. "That'll give me another chance at him. And this time, there

181

won't be a lot of his friends around him. It'll just be the two of us."

Preston and Brandt looked at Waco, who had a confused expression on his face.

"What the hell are you talking about — this time it will be just the two of you?" Brandt asked.

"Me 'n Smoke Jensen nearly had us a fight," Waco said. "Only things wasn't quite right, so I didn't draw on him."

"Is he tellin' the truth?" Brandt asked.

Manning chuckled. "Yeah, just like he said, him 'n Jensen nearly squared off."

"He didn't seem to want to fight," Waco said. "And we was standing in the middle of all his people, so I didn't push him that much."

"You don't say. Well, it's lucky for you that you didn't push him," Preston said. "Otherwise, you wouldn't be standing here right now."

"Yeah?" Waco said. "The time will come. You'll see."

One of Brandt's men came into the saloon then. He stood just inside the door, beating himself with his hat, raising a cloud of dust as he did so.

"What the hell are you doin', Arnie?" someone called. "Go outside to dust yourself off."

"That's all right," Brandt said. "Come on over."

Arnie walked over to the table where Brandt and Stone were sitting. He was no longer brushing himself off, but he was leaving little puffs of dust in the air as he walked.

"What did you see?"

"There's maybe three or four hundred head down in the south range, several miles away from anyone else," Arnie said. "I think they're gettin' ready to push them on up north to join with the herd they'll be takin' on the drive to Kansas."

Brandt smiled. "Good, good. Good work. Get yourself a beer, on me, then get ready to go back."

The expression on Arnie's face indicated that he clearly did not expect to have to go back. He had ridden twenty miles today and he was tired.

"All right," he said. "Thanks for the beer."

"Sergeant, call assembly," Brandt ordered.

"Yes, sir, Major," Stone replied in an official tone.

In an area that Captain King called the Vetadero Meadows, one of his cowboys,

Juan Arino, saw some riders moving several cattle to the south. Thinking that Ramon might have sent some men to help with the roundup, he sighed and shook his head. Whoever they were, they were undoing the work that Juan and his friends had spent the last few days doing. The cattle were supposed to be driven north, not south. What was wrong with these people?

Juan started riding toward them to see who they were, and to tell them that they were making a mistake.

He called out to them.

"Amigos. Usted está cometiendo un error. Usted debe ir con los ganado vacuno al norte!"

He yelled as loudly as he could, but his voice sounded thin in the hot wind that was blowing across the prairie. He urged his horse into a faster lope.

As he drew closer to the riders, he realized that he did not recognize any of them. These weren't Santa Gertrudis riders. Who were they, and what were they doing here on Captain King's land? Suddenly Juan had a bad feeling about this, and pulled his horse to a halt.

These men weren't making a mistake. They knew exactly what they were doing. They were rustling cattle!

Juan didn't know whether to stay and watch for a while longer, to see if he could determine where they were going with the cattle . . . or if he should get back to the others and tell them what was happening.

The decision was taken away from him when he heard the angry buzz of a bullet flying past his ear. Looking around, he saw a man, on a horse, holding a rifle to his shoulder. A white puff of smoke billowed from the end of the rifle and he watched, almost as if detached, as the shooter rocked back in his saddle from the recoil of the rifle, all in perfect silence.

"Uhnh!" he gasped as he felt the bullet go deep into his chest. It wasn't until then, as he was already tumbling from his horse, that he heard the sound of the rifle.

"Son of a bitch," Preston said, laughing, as he slid his rifle back into the saddle sheath. "Did you folks see that shot? Hell, it had to be five hundred yards at least."

Brandt rode up then. "Manning, you and Waco ride down there to where he came from and make sure there's nobody else coming," he ordered. "We've got two or three thousand dollars on the hoof here and I wouldn't want anything to happen that would keep us from collecting."

185

"All right, Major," Manning said. "Come on, Waco."

The two men rode at least three miles before they came upon a cow camp. There were three men sitting around a fire. When they heard Waco and Manning approaching, they stood and faced them.

"Quién es usted?" one of them asked. *"Dónde ser Juan?"*

"Speak English," Waco said as he swung down from his horse to face the three men. He noticed that all three men were wearing pistols.

"Who are you? Where is Juan?"

"Juan is dead," Waco answered.

"Muerto?"

"Dead, yes. And I killed him." That wasn't exactly true. It was Preston, not Waco, who shot Juan. But for Waco's purposes right now, it didn't matter who killed Juan.

"You killed him?"

"Yeah," Waco said. "What are you going to do about it?

Waco stared at the three men, a mirthless smile on his face.

It took the three men a moment to realize that they were being challenged. But how could that be? Was it possible that one man, with his pistol still in his holster, was challenging all three of them.

186

"Ahora!" one of them yelled and, as one, all three men reached for their pistols.

The smile on Waco's face actually grew broader and he watched, almost with detachment, as the three Mexicans started for their guns. He paused for just a second, then with little more than a jump in his shoulder, his gun was in his hand. He fired three times, firing so quickly that the echoes from the gunshots came back as one sustained roar.

All three Mexicans went down, mortally wounded. Not one had managed to get off a shot.

Waco held his smoking gun for a moment as he looked at the bodies of the three men he had just killed; then he twirled the gun a couple of times before putting it back in his holster. Gunsmoke from the three discharges drifted across the area, and some even wisped up from the end of the barrel at the bottom of his holster.

Waco looked up at Manning, who had watched the entire thing unfold. Manning had an expression of shock and awe on his face.

"Mr. Manning," Waco said. "No scatter-gun?"

Manning blanched in quick fear.

"You know I could kill you now, don't

187

you?" Waco said. "I could kill you, and say it was one of these boys who did it."

"I . . . I reckon you could," Manning said meekly.

Waco chuckled. "Well, don't worry. I ain't goin' to." He nodded toward the three bodies. "What did you think of that?"

"Fastest damn thing I've ever seen," Manning agreed.

"Faster'n Smoke Jensen?"

"I don't see how he could be any faster," Manning agreed.

"Are you ready to take back what you said earlier about me bein' scared of Jensen?"

"Yeah," Manning said. "Yeah, I am."

"You ain't sayin' that just 'cause you know I could kill you, are you?"

Manning shook his head. "No," he said. "I've never seen anything faster'n that."

Chapter Thirteen

Although King and his party had actually reached the ranch, they did not make it all the way back to the house on the first day of their travel. They camped out on Chilripin Creek that first evening, and the entourage was so well equipped that their supper was anything but the kind of fare one might normally expect while camping.

Two of the men traveling with the entourage were cooks, and one of the wagons was carrying a cooking stove and oven. The cooks prepared salt pork with fried apples and potatoes, sliced cucumbers, and a black walnut chess pie.

"Look at Pearlie," Cal said. "He is in hog heaven."

Pearlie didn't even hear the comment, so intent was he on the food.

During the meal, King entertained the others with the story of his past . . . which Smoke had to admit was as colorful as his own.

"I was born in New York City on July 10,

1824, to Irish parents who didn't have a pot to piss in, or a window to throw it through," King began.

"Richard!" Henrietta gasped.

King laughed. "I'm sorry, my dear, but when folks see all this" — he took in the land with a sweep of his hand — "I want them to know it wasn't given to me."

King continued his story, telling how he ran away from his indentured servitude, stowed away on a ship, and wound up buying land in Texas.

He chuckled. "But that was during my adventurous years. I've calmed down a lot since then. The most exciting thing I do now is develop new breeds of cattle."

"Yes," Smoke said. "I've heard of your Santa Gertrudis breed. They say it is one of the finest breeds of cattle around."

"It's a good breed, if I do say so myself," King said. "They are as sturdy as longhorns, as meaty as Herefords. And right now they bring top dollar at the markets."

"Which is why you are being targeted by rustlers, no doubt," Smoke said.

"Well, you would think so, wouldn't you?" King said. "But the ones who hit us didn't steal any cattle. They killed several head, but they didn't steal any."

"Why would they kill your cattle and not

take them?"

"To answer that question, you would have to understand the minds of the men who did this."

"Tell me about them," Smoke said.

"Smoke, do we have to talk about such things tonight?" Sally asked. "The food is delicious, the company good, the night is beautiful . . . couldn't we just enjoy the moment?"

"Sally's right. I didn't mean to bring up any unpleasantness," Smoke apologized.

"No, no, it's quite all right. I think it is something you should know, and there is no time better than the present to tell you about it," King said. He looked at Sally. "That is, with your permission, ma'am. The story does have its terrible moments."

Sally nodded. "Of course you can tell the story. If Smoke is going to help you, he is going to have to know as much about these people as he possibly can."

"Thank you. I will . . . uh . . . tell the story in as delicate a fashion as I can."

"Oh, nonsense," Sally replied. "Smoke will tell you, I am not faint of heart."

Smoke laughed. "She's telling the truth there," he said.

With supper finished and pipes and cigars lit, King began his story, telling of the raid against his ranch during the war.

"I suppose that the ranch was a legitimate target," he conceded. "I was running the Union blockade to sell Confederate cotton to the British . . . and I was buying arms and ammunition to sell to the South. I didn't know I had done that much for the Southern war effort, but it did catch someone's attention because we were the target of a raid by Union troops."

King paused for a few moments and took several puffs from his pipe before he went on, obviously trying to compose himself.

"Unfortunately, the leader of that attack was a man named Jack Brandt. Major Jack Brandt had a particularly nasty habit of using his sword to decapitate his victims." Again he paused. "But not until he let his men rape the women and young girls. In all, he killed twenty-three innocent men, women, and children."

"What happened to Brandt?" Smoke asked.

"He went to prison," King said. "I thought he would be hanged, or at the very least, given a life sentence."

"But he is out now?" Smoke asked, anticipating where the story was going.

"He's out," Kleberg said, answering for King. "I checked with the authorities. He and Wiley Stone were released at the same time."

"I take it Stone was one of the men with him," Smoke said.

"Yes. Stone was his sergeant," King said. He sighed. "I believe these same two men have come back to plague me," King said.

"Do you have any proof of that — that he is the one who attacked your men?" Pearlie asked.

King shook his head. "No. All I have is a gut feeling."

"I've known a lot of good men in my life," Smoke said. "And I've learned to trust their feelings. So that's good enough for me."

"I appreciate that," King said. "But what bothers me now is the fact that we are having cattle roundups back at the ranch. I've told Ramon to get as many cattle moved to the north end of the range as possible. I intend to cut ten thousand head out and drive them north."

"How long will it take you to have your roundup and get your herd under way?" Smoke asked.

"I think we should be able to get the drive started within two weeks," King said. "And during those two weeks we will be pretty vulnerable."

"Maybe we can figure out a way to make you less vulnerable," Smoke said.

"Mr. Jensen," King began.

"Please, call me Smoke."

"Smoke," King corrected. "I want you to know how much I appreciate this . . . especially when I was so dumb as to refuse to accept your help."

"Ah, think nothing of it," Smoke said. "Just consider it one rancher helping another."

Later that night, two large tents were erected, one for Richard King and his family along with Bob Kleberg, and the other for Smoke, Sally, Pearlie, and Cal. The tents were well ventilated, and furnished with canvas cots so that the occupants didn't have to sleep on the ground.

The ranch hands who were riding with the entourage slept on the ground, or in the wagon.

"Captain King is a very rich man, isn't he?" Sally asked that night as they settled into their cots.

"He's rich, I guess. But he's no richer than I am," Smoke replied.

"What?" Sally replied in surprise. "How can you say that? Captain King has thousands of acres of land . . . hundreds of thousands of acres. And who knows how many head of cattle? Now, unless Sugarloaf is a lot bigger than you have told me, Captain King is a lot richer than you are."

Smoke chuckled. "Well, my dear, I suppose it is all in how you measure wealth."

"What do you mean? How many ways are there to measure wealth?"

"Well, you could say that because I have you, and my freedom to enjoy you, that I am the wealthiest man in the world," Smoke said.

Sally gasped, then was quiet for a long moment.

"Are you all right?" Smoke asked.

"Yes," Sally answered. She was quiet for another long moment before she spoke again, her voice coming from the dark, filled with awe.

"Smoke. I do believe that is the nicest thing you have ever said to me."

In the predawn darkness, several riders appeared. Their leader held up his hand and, like the precision military formation they were, the riders came to a halt.

"There they are," Preston said, pointing.

"You are sure that is King?" Brandt asked.

"Yes," Preston said. "I seen his coach while I was in town. That's it, right there. And who else would be travelin' with a coach, three wagons, and two big tents?"

"I think you are right," Brandt said. "I believe it is King."

"What are we going to do, Major?" Stone asked.

"We're going to attack," Brandt replied.

"I thought you didn't want to kill him yet."

"Sergeant Stone, you were in the war, same as I was," Brandt replied. "You know as well as anybody that battle plans are fluid, and always subject to change."

"Yes, sir," Stone replied.

"Spread the men out and commence shooting upon my first shot," Brandt ordered.

Chapter Fourteen

Even before the fusillade that followed Brandt's signal shot, Smoke was out of his cot with his gun in hand. He heard bullets popping through the canvas wall of the tent.

"Out of your cots!" he shouted. "Everyone get down on the ground and stay low!"

By now there were so many guns being fired that the shooting made one sustained roar. In addition to the sound of the gunfire, there was the buzzing of bullets as they punched in through one side of the tent, then poked out the other side.

Smoke crawled to the edge of the tent, then lifted the canvas up from the bottom. He could see flashes in the night as a veritable army was firing toward them. He didn't know how many were out there, but from the number of flashes, and the rapidity of the firing, he knew that there were quite a few.

Smoke chose one of the flashes and, taking a chance on the shooter being right-handed, fired just to the right of the flame pattern. He didn't hear anything, nor could he see anything, but he was gratified to see that there were no more muzzle flashes emanating from that particular location.

By now, Pearlie and Cal had also poked their heads and shoulders from under the tent and, like Smoke, they were returning fire. Smoke could hear other gunshots coming from King's party, a very good demonstration coming from the cowboys who were accompanying the train, but also, he was gratified to hear shots from Captain King's tent. That meant that they were not above carrying the fight themselves.

Bullets continued to whistle through the night. Many of them made little fireballs as they struck stone, then whined off into the darkness.

The firing continued very intensely for nearly a full minute.

"Right flank, continue to put down covering fire!" Smoke heard a commanding voice shouting from the darkness. "Left flank, pull back in an orderly withdrawal!"

The incoming fire decreased by about half. Then that firing halted, to be replaced by shooting from further away. Smoke was surprised by the orderliness of the withdrawal. After a few minutes, there was no more incoming fire at all, though people within King's party were still shooting.

"Cease fire!" Smoke called. "Don't waste any more ammunition, you are shooting into the dark!"

The firing eased off, not sharply, but raggedly.

"*Cease tiroteo!*" King called. "*Cease tiroteo!*"

The last shot was fired.

"Is anyone hurt?" Smoke called into the dark.

"*Sí, señor. Mi amigo,* Vincente, he is hurt."

"I'll see to him," Sally said.

"Wait," Smoke said. "Let me check out the area first. Pearlie, you go around to our people and tell them not to move around yet. All we need now is for someone to kill one of our own people."

"What are you going to do?" Pearlie asked.

"I'm going to go out there and have a look around," Smoke said as he began poking out the spent cartridges from his cylinder and replacing them with fresh shells.

"You're the one who had better be careful then," Pearlie said.

Smoke snorted, which may have been a laugh.

"You're right," he said. "Look, stop by everyone's post. Tell them that I'm going to be out there, so don't get itchy."

"All right," Pearlie said.

"Hold up, Pearlie, I'll come with you," Cal said. "With both of us going, we can get to everyone twice as fast."

The two young men slipped through the front flap of the tent, then, running bent over, started along the line of wagons.

"Don't shoot, don't shoot!" Pearlie shouted as he approached the others. Cal was doing the same thing while running in the opposite direction.

Smoke waited until both Pearlie and Cal were gone before he slipped out under the tent wall. He crawled through rocks, sand, and various types of cactus — his way covered by darkness — closing his mind to the pricks and stabs of everything from sharp-edged stone to long, very pointed cactus needles.

As Smoke moved through the night toward where he had heard the sound of guns, he could see puffs of white gun smoke hanging in the black night air over where the raiders had been. He could also smell the acrid bitterness of burnt powder.

He moved closer, his unobserved approach as silent as the moon shadows. Then, by the light of the moon, he saw two men waiting, staring toward the King encampment. The pullback had been a ruse.

"Did you two men get left behind, or what?" Smoke called out.

"What the hell?" one of them shouted in alarm. Both men turned toward Smoke and fired; though, as Smoke had moved after he called out to them, they were shooting toward the sound of where his voice had been.

Smoke had a better target, and it took him only two shots to take care of both of them. As soon as he fired, he moved from his location again, knowing that the muzzle flashes would give him away to anyone else who might be hiding out. There was no more shooting, but Smoke remained quietly in his new location, sheltered behind a rock, hidden by the deep shadows of predawn darkness.

Gradually, the black turned to gray . . . then the first pink fingers of dawn touched the mesquite, and the light was soft and the air was cool. The last morning star made a bright pinpoint of light over a line of mountains, lying in a ragged line far to the west.

A rustle of wind through feathers caused him to look up just in time to see a golden eagle diving on its prey. The eagle swooped back into the air, carrying a tiny desert mouse kicking fearfully in the eagle's claws. A Gila monster scurried beneath a nearby mesquite tree, which was itself dying under the burden of parasitic mistletoe.

Smoke stayed where he was. Then, as the sun reached two fingers above the eastern horizon, nearly every shadow was eliminated and he could see two bodies lying on the ground. Then something caught his eye . . . a movement behind a low-lying mesquite tree. He saw someone raise up and aim a rifle, and when Smoke looked in the direction the man was aiming, he saw that Alice King was standing just outside the King tent.

The son of a bitch was about to shoot a woman!

"Drop that gun!" Smoke called.

Instead of dropping his rifle, the man swung it toward Smoke and fired. The bullet was uncomfortably close, so close that it actually left a burn mark on Smoke's neck. Smoke returned fire, and the man threw up his rifle as he tumbled backward.

Smoke waited for a long moment before he exposed himself again. Then he heard someone coming and, with gun drawn, he swung toward him.

"No, Smoke, it's me!" Pearlie shouted in alarm.

"I told you to stay back there," Smoke said gruffly. He was angry and frightened that he had almost shot Pearlie.

"We heard all the shooting," Pearlie said. "Miss Sally was going to come check on you herself. The only way I could get her to stay back was to promise her that I would do it."

Smoke's irritation dissipated. He knew how hard it was to resist Sally once she made her mind up to something. He smiled. "Well, as you can see, I'm all right."

Pearlie looked around at the bodies lying on the ground.

"Yeah, well, that's more than we can say about these fellas, isn't it?"

"Yeah," Smoke said. "I'll say this for them. They were determined. Come on, let's get back. Unless you think someone might shoot us as we come in."

"I told 'em to look for me at that rock over there," Pearlie said, pointing toward a rather large rock.

"Good idea to tell them where to expect us," Smoke said.

It took no more than a couple of minutes to return to the encampment, where Sally greeted Smoke with a welcoming kiss that was almost embarrassing in its intensity. He winced when she wrapped her arms around his neck, and startled by his reaction, Sally drew back to examine his wound.

"You were hit!" Sally said.

Smoke put his hand up to his neck. "Just a graze, no blood," he said. "It left me with a burn, like a rope burn."

"Let me put some cold cream on it," she said.

As the two tents were struck, Smoke sat on a wagon tongue, letting Sally apply cold cream to his wound. King came over to talk to him.

"We heard a little activity out there this morning," King said.

"Yes. Three of them were left back. I think the plan was to open up on us, once we thought we were safe and under way again."

"Where are the three now?" King asked.

"They're still out there," Smoke said. "But I don't think they will be bothering anyone again."

"No, I don't suppose they will either. By chance, none of them was wearing an Army jacket, was he?

"No," Smoke said.

"Too bad."

Smoke saw that Vincente had been tended to, and was now sitting up with his shirt off and a bandage wrapped around his upper arm.

"How is he?" Smoke said, nodding toward the wounded man.

"He'll be fine, if he doesn't get the gangrene," King said.

"Was he the only man we have who was wounded?" Smoke asked.

"Yes. But we lost a couple of horses," King said.

"By the way, I do believe you when you say that this man Brandt is the one behind all this."

"You do? You saw him?"

Smoke shook his head. "No, I didn't see him."

King looked confused. "Then what makes you think he is the one behind all this?"

"I think this because of the way they withdrew this morning," Smoke said. "I clearly heard the order for one half of the men to provide cover while the other half of the men pulled back. It was a very precise maneuver. Add to that the fact that they set up an ambush and it makes me think the person we are dealing with has a military background."

"Major Jack Brandt," King said.

"I think you are right," Smoke replied.

"Three men killed!" Brandt said. "We surprise an encampment of civilians in the middle of the night, and we had three men killed? We should have killed all of them without so much as a scratch, but we were lucky to get out alive."

"Yeah," Preston said.

"You want to tell me just how the hell that happened? It was the perfect ambush plan. What could possibly have gone wrong?"

"Well, we was waitin' back there, like you said, waitin' for daylight so's we could pick 'em off when they started out. Only he come out in the night to find us. It's like he knew we was goin' to be out there."

"He came out," Brandt said. "Who came out?"

"Jensen. Smoke Jensen," Preston said. "You know. He's the one I told you about."

"How many men did he bring out with him?" Brandt asked.

"He didn't bring nobody with him. It was just him," Preston said.

"Well, if he came out all by himself, why didn't you kill him when you had a chance?"

"You don't understand," Preston said.

"What is it I don't understand?"

"He's not like just one man. Fact is, he's not like anything I've ever seen before. We never really got a chance to kill him," Preston replied. "I mean, Dewey and

Houston, they got themselves kilt right off. Then Evans, he got hisself kilt right after first light. That left me as the only one."

"How is it you weren't killed?" Brandt asked.

" 'Cause I wasn't about to show myself," Preston said. "Like I told you, by then I was the only one left. Any man who would go up ag'in Smoke Jensen all by hisself is a damn fool."

"Who is Smoke Jensen anyway? I've never even heard of him," Brandt said.

"He's just one of the most famous gunfighters there is, is all," Preston said. "How can it possibly be that you have never heard of him? Why, they've even wrote dime novels about him."

"I was in prison for over fifteen years," Brandt said. "We didn't get a lot of dime novels in prison."

"Well, take my word for it, Major. Smoke Jensen ain't somebody you want to run up against alone."

"I'm not afraid of him," Waco said. "I'll face him alone."

"Really?" Brandt said, his voice dripping with sarcasm.

"You damn right I would."

"Now, why would you want to do that?" Brandt asked.

"Why, to prove that I am better than he is," Waco said.

"I am running a military organization here," Brandt said. "I am not running a competition of personal accomplishments. I don't care whether you are better than he is or not. You do understand that, don't you?"

"Well, yes, sure I understand that," Waco replied. "I mean, I guess I understand it. But if you're worried about me gettin' killed or . . ."

"I'm not worried about you getting killed," Brandt said. "Individually, you mean nothing. Collectively, you are part of my army, and I don't want my army weakened, even by one more."

"Yeah, but if someone would just take care of Smoke Jensen for you, you could . . ."

"You do want to stay with us, don't you, Jones?"

"Yes. Of course I do."

"Then, not another word about you and this man Smoke Jensen having your own personal battle. A pretty good general for the other side once said that you win battles by getting their 'fustest with the mostest.' That is the principle by which I am running this organization. We will win all of our battles with overwhelming military superiority . . . not with some brash young fool out to make a name for himself. You will make no effort to face this man by yourself."

"All right," Waco said. "But I just want you to know, I want everyone to know," he emphasized, looking directly at Manning, "that I am not afraid of Smoke Jensen."

Brandt sighed. "You are an idiot," he said. "An absolute idiot."

Waco seethed at Brandt's words, but he knew there was nothing he could do about it. Even though he could draw his pistol and kill Brandt in a heartbeat, he was surrounded by nearly a dozen of Brandt's men. This was a vivid example of Brandt's principle of overwhelming military superiority.

Chapter Fifteen

When the King entourage turned up the long road that led to the main house, they were greeted with a large sign.

LAS PERSONAS DE SANTA GERTRUDIS
RANCH DAN LA
BIENVENIDA AL CAPITÁN KING DE CASA

"What's that sign say?" Cal asked.

"It's the people of the ranch welcoming Captain King home," Pearlie said.

"Really? You can read Mexican?"

"It's Spanish, not Mexican."

As the coach rolled up the road, Sally looked through the window at those who were gathered to welcome them back. Men and women stood respectfully along the road. The men had all removed their hats and were holding them in front of their chests. Many of the women curtsied as the coach passed by. Children and dogs ran alongside the coach, keeping pace with it until it stopped in front of the house.

Sally started to reach for the door but something told her to wait, and a moment later the door was opened from outside, disclosing a weathered, gray-haired man.

"Welcome home, Señora, Señorita," the gray-haired man said.

"Thank you, Pablo," Henrietta said as she offered her hand to him to be helped down from the coach.

Sally started to wait for Alice but, with a warm smile, Alice made a motion with her hand, indicating that Sally should go before her.

When Sally stepped out, she looked over to see Smoke, Captain King, and Kleberg engaged in serious conversation with someone. The expressions on their faces were not happy.

"I wonder what happened while we were gone," Henrietta asked. "Ramon looks very worried."

Sally was glad to see that her intuition wasn't wrong. Something had happened, and even Henrietta had noticed it.

"It's Juan Arino and the others we sent down to Vetadero Meadows," Ramon said. "They are dead."

"How many are dead?"

"Everyone we sent down there," Juan said.

"Numbers, man, I want numbers," King said impatiently.

"Four."

King sighed, pinched the bridge of his nose, then shook his head. "That makes a total of twelve," he said. "Twelve good men killed, just because Brandt has some personal score to settle with me. Damn it! Why the hell won't he come out and face me in person?"

"Were the men decapitated?" Kleberg asked.

Ramon shook his head. "No, Señor."

"Did they take any cattle?"

"*Sí, señor.* They took all the cattle in the Vetadero Meadows. About three hundred head."

"Richard, are you sure this was Brandt?" Kleberg asked. "No beheadings, and they took cattle. This is different from the last time."

"It is him," King insisted. "I don't care whether he is doing things differently or not. I know, as sure as I am standing here, that it was either Jack Brandt, or someone who is working for Jack Brandt."

Nearly ten miles away from the main house, Ted Abbot, Roy Carter, Emil Barrett, and Bobby Spitz were on horseback, moving alongside a meandering creek. They had been out for four days, taking a tally of the cattle that weren't with the main herd.

One of the problems with Santa Gertrudis was that the ranch was so large, and there were so many head of cattle, that it was easy to lose count of how many head there actually were. It was nearly a full-time job for cowboys to ride around the perimeter of the ranch, locating the maverick herds.

"Whoa, stop here," Carter said.

"What for?" Barrett asked.

Carter swung down from his horse. "I've gotta water the lilies," he said.

The other three remained in their saddles while Carter went about his business; then they heard him laugh.

"What are you laughin' at?" Spitz asked.

"I just peed me a grasshopper off'n that branch there," Carter said. "You should'a seen him, he was hangin' on for dear life, but I peed him right off."

"You must be very proud," Barrett said, and the other three men laughed.

"Hey, Cap'n King is supposed to get back today, ain't he?" Carter asked as he remounted.

"Yes, I think so," Barrett said.

"He ain't goin' to like it when he hears

about Juan and them others," Carter said as he clucked his horse on.

The four rode in relative silence for about another mile. Then Carter saw three riders, pushing about twenty head of cattle. He pointed them out to the others.

"Look down there," he said. "Them ain't Santa Gertrudis riders, are they?"

"Ain't none that I know," Spitz said.

"Maybe we ought to go down there and see what's goin' on."

"I don't know," Barrett said hesitantly. "I mean, if they are rustling cattle, it might not be a good idea to just ride in on them."

"Come on, there are three of them, there are four of us," Spitz said.

"Bobby is right," Carter said. "Let's go down there and see what's goin' on."

The four rode toward the three men who were pushing the cattle, urging their horses, not into a gallop, but a ground-eating trot. Because the three riders were paying attention to the cows, and because of the sound of their horses' hoofbeats, they did not hear anyone coming up on them. As the four cowboys approached a rather dense thicket, Carter indicated they should go on the left as the cattle passed by on the right. That gave them the opportunity to overtake the three men and then, on the other side of the thicket, suddenly appear in front of them.

And that is exactly what they did, startling the three riders.

"Hold it!" Carter shouted.

The three riders were stopped by the challenge.

"Who the hell are you?" Carter asked.

"Who the hell are you?" the youngest of the three riders replied.

"We're riders for the Santa Gertrudis Ranch."

"Santa Gertrudis Ranch?" the youngest rider said. He shook his head. "Nope, I've never heard of it."

"That's funny," Carter said.

"What's funny about it?"

"You're on the Santa Gertrudis right now," Carter said. He pointed to the cattle. "And them are Santa Gertrudis cows."

"There's no brand on these cows," the young rider said.

"That don't matter none. You can't . . . what did you say your name was?" Carter asked.

"My name is Jones. Waco Jones."

"Jones. Well, Jones, you can't come onto another man's ranch an' start roundin' up his cattle just 'cause they ain't been branded yet. That ain't no better'n stealin'."

Waco smiled, a cold, evil smile. "Well," he said, "I reckon you called it, 'cause stealin' is what we're doin', all right."

Carter was surprised by Waco Jones's response. He'd as much as admitted that they were rustling cattle.

"My God, mister! You admit that you're stealin' cattle?"

"Yep. What are you goin' to do about it?" Waco asked.

"Well, I don't intend to let you get away with it," Carter said, reaching for his gun.

"Carter, no, don't draw!" Abbot shouted. "Shit!" he yelled, going for his own gun to support Carter.

Waco's draw was unbelievably fast. He fired two times before either Carter or Abbot could pull the triggers on their guns; then, even as they were tumbling from their saddles, Waco turned his gun toward Spitz and Barrett.

"No!" Barrett shouted, putting his hands up. "We ain't drawing on you!"

Waco held his gun pointed toward them for a long moment, smiling at his enjoyment of their fear. Then he put his pistol back in his holster.

"What is my name?" Waco asked.

"What?" Spitz asked in a weak voice.

"What is my name?" Waco asked again.

"I . . . I don't know your name," Spitz said. "And he don't either," he added, nodding toward Barrett. "So there ain't no way the law is goin' to find out who done this."

"What is my name?" Waco asked again, more pointedly this time.

Spitz looked at Waco with an expression of confusion and fear.

"I'll be damned," Barrett said, suddenly realizing what Waco was doing. "He wants us to tell." Barrett stared at Waco. "That's it, isn't it? You want us to tell."

"The name is Waco Jones," Waco said. "Do you have that? Waco Jones."

"Yeah," Barrett said. "I've got it."

"Now, if you boys will excuse us, we'll just take these unbranded cows on," Waco said.

"We'll be takin' our friends on back, if you don't mind," Barrett said, pointing to Carter and Abbot. Both men were sprawled on the ground.

Waco nodded, and Barrett and Spitz put the two bodies belly-down across the dead men's horses, using their own ropes to secure them. Once the bodies were loaded, they rode off while Waco and the two with him continued driving the cattle. "We just going to let them get away with it?" Spitz asked, his anger barely controlled.

"What do you propose we do about it?" Barrett asked.

"I don't know. But it just galls me to see them get away with it."

"Did you say Waco Jones?" Smoke asked.

"That's what he said his name was," Barrett said. "And he was real anxious that we remember it too."

Smoke nodded. "Yes, he's just the kind that would want you to remember it."

"You should have killed the son of a bitch when you had the chance," Pearlie said.

Smoke looked at Pearlie, but he didn't say anything, because he knew that Pearlie was right.

Chapter Sixteen

On the day after Smoke arrived, Captain King called a meeting of all his hands, leaving a bare minimum to keep watch over his herds. They gathered in front of the big house, Americans and Mexicans alike, wondering what this was about.

Because of the size of the ranch, and the vastness of the operation, many of the men had not seen each other in quite a while. They shook hands and used the opportunity to visit and catch up on the latest news. The cooks came out to pass around coffee and sinkers and it took on the atmosphere of a party with laughter prevailing. But when Captain King came out on the porch, the men grew silent, out of respect, but also out of curiosity.

"Men," King said. "I know that you know about the troubles we have been having lately. So far we have had fourteen of our men murdered."

"Fourteen?" someone said, and there was a murmur through the assembly as they contemplated that fact.

"We've had some cows stolen too, haven't we, Cap'n?" another asked.

"Yes, we've had some cattle stolen, but I don't care about that. What I *do* care about is the men we have lost, and I intend to put a stop to that."

"How?" one of the men asked.

Some of the others glared at him.

"Don't you boys look at me like that," King said. "I was out there when them fellers hit us the first time. They was like an army ridin' through. Hell, they *was* an army. We're going to be an army too. And we have just the man to lead us. Men, I want you to meet Smoke Jensen."

Smoke had been waiting just inside the house, and he came out onto the front porch when King said his name.

Several of the men had heard of Smoke Jensen, and there were several comments passed back and forth.

"Damn, if that is the real Smoke Jensen, we are going to kick some ass," someone said. There was a smattering of laughter, though the laughter quieted as Smoke began to speak.

"Gentlemen, am I correct in assuming that you are ready to fight back next time something happens?"

"Yes!" Barrett shouted, and the others echoed his yell.

"Is there anyone here who does not have a gun?"

Three of the Mexican riders raised their hands, and Smoke glanced toward King.

"I will supply you with guns," King said. "And I will supply ammunition for everyone."

"All right, men, let's get started," Smoke said.

For the next few days, only a minimum work force was kept in the field to tend the cattle. Everyone else stayed back at the ranch headquarters, where they were trained by Smoke, Pearlie, and Cal.

When someone commented that Cal seemed a little young to be training grown men, Smoke asked Cal to give them a demonstration.

Cal put a skillet on the ground, then held his hand out in front of him palm-down. On the back of his hand was a heavy metal washer. Smoke put a bottle on a fence post, then nodded at Cal.

Cal turned his hand and the washer slid off, falling toward the skillet. Cal pulled his pistol and shot, breaking the bottle, before the washer hit the skillet.

Those who watched the demonstration applauded.

"That's good," Barrett said. "But that don't mean you can teach us to be that good."

Sally had been watching the demonstration and, when Barrett made his comment, Smoke called out to her.

"Sally, you want to show what I taught you?" he asked.

"I don't have time for this," Sally said. "I've got some bear claws in the oven."

"Oh, you have time for this," Smoke said.

"All right," Sally replied. "Let me get my pistol."

"You can use mine, Miss Sally," Pearlie said. "I wouldn't want nothin' to happen to them bear claws."

Sally glared at Pearlie.

"I mean, I wouldn't want anything to happen to *those* bear claws," he said to correct himself.

"That's more like it," Sally said as she took Pearlie's gun and spun the cylinder, checking the loads.

"Is she going to do a fast draw too?" Spitz asked.

"I don't do fast draw," Sally said.

"Being able to draw fast is good for show," Smoke said. "But the kind of fighting you will be doing will have nothing at all to do with drawing fast, and everything to do with hitting what you are shooting at."

Smoke picked up three bottles and held them in his hand, then looked over at Sally. She nodded, and brought the pistol up to ready.

"When you come up against more than one target, the trick is not to get confused, but to choose a target that you know you can hit."

Smoke tossed all three bottles into the air at the same time. The gun in Sally's hand roared three times and, after each shot, a bottle burst. Little bits of shattered glass rained to the ground, but not one whole bottle.

The applause was instantaneous and enthusiastic.

"I thought you said to select the target you thought you could hit," Spitz said.

"I did," Sally said, smiling, as she handed the gun back to Pearlie.

The men laughed.

"Now," Smoke said when the laughter died down. "Are you men ready to learn?"

The response was an enthusiastic "Yes!"

Smoke designed a training course consisting of target practice for both pistol and rifle. For the next few days, the area around Casa Grande reverberated with the steady firing of weapons, shouts from the men, and galloping hoofbeats as the men rode at full speed through difficult obstacle courses.

After a week of training, he had a pretty good idea of what he was working with. He began to divide the men into smaller groups, sometimes reassigning a man from one group to another. When King asked why he was doing that, Smoke explained that he was trying to get each group balanced as to capabilities.

"I don't want all the best shots together," he said. "And I don't want all the best horsemen together. I also want someone with leadership who can take charge of each group so that, if they encounter the raiders, he can determine the best course of action."

"Yes," King said, nodding. "Yes, I can see that. That's a good idea."

"In a couple more days, I believe we will have as effective an army as Brandt," Smoke said.

"I agree," King replied. "You have done splendid work. Oh, and speaking of armies, maybe it's time I showed you something," he added mysteriously.

"What?"

"They are down there, behind a false wall

at the back of the machine shed," King said, pointing to a building about fifty yards away from the main house.

"Now, you do have me curious," Smoke said as he walked with King to the ripsawed, unpainted, and sun-grayed wood-sided building.

Once inside, King got a crowbar and began prying out a nail. The nail squeaked in protest as he started pulling it from the dried wood.

"Keep in mind that, during the war, I often supplied the Confederate Army with arms and munitions," King said.

"Yes, I remember you telling me. You want me to help you with that?"

"No, I'm just going to pull a couple of nails so we can pull the board out to let you look behind," King answered.

He pulled a second nail, then, when both nails were removed, grabbed the board and pulled it out at the bottom, just opening up enough space for Smoke to look through.

Smoke put his eye to the crack and looked inside.

"Holy shit!" he said with a low whistle.

"I thought you might be impressed," King said. "You know what they say. Artillery lends dignity to what would otherwise be an uncouth brawl."

There, behind the false wall, were two caisson-mounted Napoleon 32-pounder cannons.

"I also have powder and ball for them," King said. "And that's not all."

"You have more of these?"

"No, not these, something else," King responded. "Come."

At the other end of the machine shed were two rather large objects covered with tarpaulin. King took the tarpaulin off one of them.

"Damn! You have a Gatling gun?" Smoke asked in surprise.

"Actually, I have two of them," King said. "With ammunition."

"Damn," Smoke said with a chuckle. "With you supplying them, how did the South lose the war?"

"I've asked myself that same question a few times," King admitted.

The next day the reshuffled groups went out on the range. Although Smoke had balanced all the groups fairly well, he sent Pearlie and Cal with the two that he thought were the weakest. The effect of their presence was immediate, elevating those two groups to the best.

Barrett's group was the first to get its

test under fire. They had been out less than a day when they saw a group of men heading toward an isolated part of the herd.

"What do we do now?" one of the men asked.

Barrett was snaking his rifle from his saddle holster even as he was answering the question.

"Shoot the sons of bitches," he said, levering a bullet into the chamber of his Winchester. "I've run across these bastards twice before. This time I'm not going to give them the first shot."

Barrett fired, and one of the rustlers grabbed his shoulder. The other cowboys began firing as well and they started toward the rustlers in full pursuit.

The rustlers, caught off guard by the rapid and effective resistance, turned and began galloping off. Barrett kept up the pursuit until the rustlers were well away, and only then did he hold up his hand and call for a halt.

Barrett looked at the men with him, then smiled broadly.

"You did well," he said proudly.

Two days later there was another incident, this time with the group that Pearlie led. Eight rustlers tried to sneak in, riding bent over on their horses as they worked their way up through a long gulley.

The raiders, shocked by the sudden appearance of Pearlie and his men, fired, then turned and tried to run. Pearlie and his men opened fire and two of the raiders fell. Then, one of Pearlie's men was hit and Pearlie called a halt to the chase to tend to his wounded.

Both raiders were dead.

Chapter Seventeen

"Let me make the next raid, Major," Stone said. He shook his head. "The last two raiding parties we've sent out have come back with their tails tucked between their legs."

Stone and Brandt were sitting at their regular table in the Gato Rojo Saloon.

"I don't know," Brandt said. He picked up the bottle to pour himself another glass of whiskey, but the bottle was empty. Kunz, ever the efficient businessman, was there instantly to replace the bottle.

"Captain King has been training his men," Kunz said as he put the bottle on the table.

Brandt looked up at him. "What do you mean, he's been training his men?"

"Several of the Mexicans who live in this town have relatives who work at the Santa Gertrudis. Word has gotten back that the gunman he hired, this man Smoke Jensen, has been training them, just like you would an army."

"Well, I'll be damn," Brandt said. He rubbed his disfigured eyelid with his forefinger. "An army, huh?"

Kunz poured the liquor into Brandt's glass. "Well, that's what the Mexicans are saying. But if you live down here long enough, you know you can never believe anything a Mexican tells you."

"I don't know," Brandt said. He took a swallow of his drink. "It makes sense when you think about it."

"So, he's got an army," Stone said. "We've fought armies before, me'n you."

"Yes, but I remind you that we had an army behind us," Brandt said. "Not a bunch of ragtag outlaws who are all out for themselves."

"What do you think we should do? Think maybe we should have one big raid? Maybe against the house?"

"We can't do anything until we have more information," Brandt said. "I need to send someone to find out. The only problem is, I'm not sure where to send him."

"Benevadis," Kunz said.

"Why Benevadis?"

"That's the closest town to the ranch and it's where all the cowboys from Santa Gertrudis go. And because there are a lot more Americans there than here, you could send someone there without raising too much suspicion."

"Thanks," Brandt said. "That's good to know."

"Happy to help, Major," Kunz replied as he started back toward the bar.

"Why?" Stone called out to him.

Kunz stopped, but he didn't turn around, nor did he answer Stone.

"Yeah, that's a good question," Brandt said. "Before I act on any information you give me, I would like to know why you are helping."

Kunz put an obsequious smile on his lips, then turned to face the two men who were now the most important people in all of Concepcion.

"Why, you ask?"

"Yeah, why? I mean, let's face it, we've run roughshod over everyone else in town . . . over your neighbors. So, why are you happy to help us?"

"Are you kidding, Major? Look around you. I've never had business this good. And no matter what you are doing to everyone else, you and your men have been straight with me. Seems only fitting that I be straight with you."

Brandt nodded. "All right," he said. "I'll accept that."

Kunz kept the smile on his face until he turned back around and started toward the bar. At that moment his face registered complete relief that he had come up with an answer that satisfied Brandt. Kunz was playing with fire, and he knew it.

"So," Stone said, continuing his conversation with Brandt. "You want me to go to Benevadis and have a look around to see what I can find out?"

Brandt shook his head. "No," he said. "I need you here. I'll think of someone."

"We could send Waco," Stone suggested.

Again, Brandt shook his head. "No, I don't want to send him. He's much too hotheaded to be dependable. We'll have to come up with someone else."

"Shit! How do you do that with just three fingers?" someone asked from one of the other tables. His question was met with a raucous round of laughter from all the others at that table.

Looking toward the laughter, Brandt saw Three-Finger Manning performing some sleight-of-hand tricks with a silver dollar.

"It's easy if you know what you are doing," Manning said. He held the dollar between the thumb and forefinger of his Three-Finger hand, then passed his other hand in front. The coin disappeared and al-

232

most immediately, he turned his good hand over to show that it wasn't there.

"That's the damnedest thing I've ever seen," Preston said.

"There's our man," Brandt said, pointing to Manning.

Smoke had not left the ranch since he arrived, so when Kleberg invited him to go with him into Benevadis, Smoke jumped at the chance.

"Did it ever occur to you that I might like to go into town?" Sally asked when Smoke told her of his plans.

"Oh, honey, you don't want to go into Benevadis," Henrietta said. She shook her head. "It's much too rough a place for a lady like you."

Sally started to respond, and Smoke could tell by the expression on her face that she was going to point out to Henrietta that she wasn't quite the "delicate" lady she appeared. But a warning glance from Smoke stopped her, though Smoke's glance was ameliorated by a smile.

Sally walked out front with Smoke. Kleberg was over in front of the barn saddling his horse. Stormy was already saddled.

"Thanks," Smoke said.

"Thanks for what?"

Smoke chuckled. "You know for what. For not spoiling Henrietta's illusion about your . . ." He paused and stared pointedly at her. "What was it you called it back in Colorado? Your female decorum?"

Sally laughed, then hit Smoke on the shoulder. "You are awful," she said.

About that time Kleberg had his horse saddled, and he rode over to Smoke.

"Are you ready to go?" he asked.

"I'm ready," Smoke replied.

"Oh?" Sally said, lifting her eyebrows. "Are you really ready?"

Smiling, Smoke kissed her.

"Now," she said, when their lips parted. "You are ready."

Benevadis was the closest town to the Santa Gertrudis Ranch, and although it, like all the other small towns around the ranch, was predominantly Mexican, Benevadis had considerably more Americans than the others. In fact, it was almost half and half. It was this demographic makeup that made Benevadis the destination of choice for most of the Americans in the area, whether they worked on the Santa Gertrudis or one of the other ranches.

Even the architecture of the little town reflected its split personality. One side of the street was American, lined with false-fronted buildings thrown together, washed out and flyblown. The first structure Smoke and Kleberg rode by was a blacksmith's shop. From the blacksmith's shop, going down on the same side of the street, was a butcher shop, a general store, a bakery, six small houses, then a leather-goods shop next door to an apothecary. A set of outside stairs climbed the left side of the drugstore to a small stoop that stuck out from the second floor. A painted hand on a sign, with a finger pointing up, read:

W. W. WEST, M.D.

After that came a saloon. On the opposite side of the street the buildings were constructed of adobe, with red tile roofs. Here was a cantina, a seamstress, a Roman Catholic church, a restaurant, and a few houses.

"You can go on down to the Hog Lot if you'd like," Kleberg said, pointing toward the saloon that bore that unlikely name in front. "I have some business to take care of with the blacksmith. I'll join you in a few minutes."

"All right," Smoke said.

Kleberg dismounted and was met by a smiling blacksmith who was wiping his hands on his apron as he approached. Smoke rode on down to the far end of the street, stopping in front of the saloon. Tying off Stormy at the hitching rail, he stepped inside the saloon, moving quickly, as he always did, to one side of the door, then stepping back against the wall.

He recognized many of the men because they were the same Santa Gertrudis riders he had been working with for the last several days.

"Hey," Spitz said. "There's Smoke."

"Smoke, over here. Let us buy you a beer!" Barrett called.

After scanning the entire saloon and determining that there was nobody there to pose a threat, Smoke smiled at the greeting and went over to join the others.

"Barkeep, a beer for our friend," Spitz said.

"Coming right up," the bartender said, sticking a mug under a barrel and pulling the lever. The mug filled with an amber liquid, then formed a two-inch foam on top. He handed it to Smoke, then took the nickel from Spitz.

"Thanks," Smoke said as he blew the foam off the head.

"I was tellin' the boys about our little run-in with the rustlers the other day," Barrett said. He went back to his story. "So, here we were, the bullets flying by, *zing, zing, zing,*" he mimicked, using his fingers to show the flight of the bullets.

"So what did you do next?" one of the others said.

"Well, I did just like Smoke here taught us," Barrett said. "I put the reins in my teeth" — he lifted the rawhide string that hung from his hat and bit down on it in demonstration — "then I filled both hands with guns and started firing away. *Bang, bang, bang,*" he said, marking each shot with his hands, formed into the shapes of pistols.

At that moment, Manning came into the saloon and, seeing everyone gathered around the talker, he moved, unobserved, to the far end of the bar. He started to call the bartender down to him when he noticed the tall man drinking the beer.

Damn! That's Smoke Jensen!

Manning moved slightly to put several people between him and the gunfighter. He didn't know if Jensen would remember him from the encounter at the dance. After all, it was Waco who'd challenged Jensen. Still, he'd rather not take any chances.

He listened to the loudmouth telling his story, realizing that he must be talking about an encounter with some of Brandt's men.

"By now," Barrett said, "bullets were flying both ways. *Bang, zing, bang, zing.*"

"Oh, man, I wish I'd been there," one of the other cowboys said. "That sounds excitin'."

"It was exciting all right. But also scary. Remember, this is the third time I've run into them fellas," Barrett said. "But this time they bit off more'n they could chew when they messed with Emil Barrett," he said, pointing to his chest with his thumb. "I mean, we must'a killed, oh, I don't know, six or seven at least. Hell, more'n that, because I got that many myself."

Suddenly Spitz laughed out loud. "Barrett, you are as full of shit as a Christmas goose," he said. "In the first place, I've never known you to carry two pistols. And as clumsy as you are on a horse, you prob'ly couldn't even stay on holdin' the reins in your teeth."

"Damn, Spitz, you do know how to mess up a good story, don't you?" Barrett complained, and Smoke and the others laughed.

Spitz turned toward the bartender, then pointed to Smoke. "I'll bet you don't know who this is, do you?" he asked.

"No, sir. I've never had the pleasure of meeting the gentleman," the bartender replied.

"Well, sir, this here is Smoke Jensen,"

Spitz said proudly. "I reckon you've heard of him, haven't you? Purt' near ever'body's heard of Smoke Jensen."

"Indeed I have, sir," the bartender replied. He looked at Smoke with an expression of awe. "Are you really Smoke Jensen?" he asked.

Smoke felt somewhat embarrassed by all the attention, and he shot Spitz a glance that let him know he didn't appreciate it. Chastised, Spitz looked away.

Smoke nodded. "Yes, I'm Smoke Jensen," he admitted with a sigh.

"Well, sir, I am really pleased to meet you," the bartender said. He wiped his hand with his apron, then extended it. "May I shake your hand?"

Smoke hesitated just for a moment, then smiled and extended his own hand. That was when, out of the corner of his eye, he saw someone at the far end of the bar suddenly go for his gun.

"Draw, Jensen!" the man shouted as he pulled his pistol.

Jerking his hand back from the bartender, Smoke drew his gun and fired at about the same time the man at the end of the bar did. The two gunshots sounded as one, and puffs of smoke billowed out from the ends of the gun barrels.

At about the same time the two shots were being fired, Spitz, Barrett, the bartender, and everyone else in the saloon were scrambling hard to get out of the way.

The bullet that was fired at Smoke was close, very close. It smashed the beer mug Smoke had put down, then it plowed into the top of the bar, sending up a shower of splinters.

The bullet from Smoke's gun hit Manning high in the chest, knocking him back against the wall. Manning looked at Smoke with an expression of surprise on his face, then slid down to the floor, leaving a track of blood on the wall behind him. He hit the floor, but remained in the sitting position. His arms flopped out to either side, with the pistol, still smoking, dangling by the trigger guard from his index finger.

"I can't believe I tried that," Manning gasped.

"Who are you?" Smoke asked. "Why did you try to shoot me?"

"I figured you might recognize me," Manning said. "And if you did, it would be too late."

"Recognize you? From where? Have we ever met?" Smoke asked, surprised by the response.

"Sort of. It was at the dance in Corpus . . ."

"You were the other one," Smoke said, suddenly remembering and interrupting him. "You were the sensible one. Or at least, I thought you were. What got into you, man? What on earth made you pull on me like you did?"

"I seen you shaking the bartender's hand and I figured that would give me just enough of an edge."

Manning coughed, and flecks of blood sprayed from his mouth.

"Somebody get a doctor," someone said.

Manning tried to chuckle, though the chuckle turned into another blood-producing cough. "Ain't no need 'a that," he said. "I'm done for. I know it 'n you know it."

"Who are you?" Smoke asked.

"The name is Manning." The shooter held up his left hand, showing that it had only three fingers. "But some folks just call me Three-Finger."

"Why did you try to kill me, Manning?"

" 'Cause that little pissant Waco Jones is always braggin' as to how he is goin' to kill you. I figured if I did it first, it would shut him up. So I took a gamble."

"Wasn't a very good gamble," Smoke said.

"No, I don't reckon it was," Manning

said. He chuckled again, though this time the chuckle was harder to manage. "Do me a favor, will you? If you see Waco, tell him I'll be waitin' for him in hell."

The doctor and the sheriff came in then, arriving at about the same time.

They were too late. Manning was dead.

Chapter Eighteen

Manning had not gone to Benevadis alone. Leon Pettis made the ride with him, and he was as shocked as anyone else when Manning suddenly drew his gun against Smoke Jensen. Pettis stayed away from Manning as he was dying, afraid that Manning might see him and say something to him that would let everyone else know that they were together. And he instinctively knew that this wasn't the place to be seen with Manning.

Pettis waited until most of the crowd had gathered around Manning's body, then left the saloon, mounted his horse, and left town, covering the fourteen miles to Concepcion in just over an hour. It was late afternoon when he got there. Waco was sitting in front of the Gato Rojo playing a solitary game of mumblety-peg on the wooden porch. He looked up when Pettis dismounted. The horse was breathing hard, and lathered in the white foam of sweat.

"Son of a bitch, Pettis, look at your

horse," Waco said. "What'd you ride him so hard for?"

"I need to talk to the major," Pettis said. "Is he inside?"

Waco glanced toward the batwing doors and nodded. "Yep, same as always," he said. "Him 'n Sarge are back there sittin' at their table."

Pettis tied off his horse.

"Hey, didn't Manning go with you?" Waco asked.

"Yeah."

Waco chuckled. "What'd you do, have a race back with that old Three-Finger fool? How far back is he?"

"He's dead," Pettis called over his shoulder as he pushed through the swinging doors.

"What?" Waco shouted, picking up his knife and getting to his feet as he followed Pettis inside.

Pettis went straight to the bar and ordered a whiskey, then tossed it down and ordered another before he turned to face Brandt.

"What do you mean he's dead? How did it happen?" Waco asked. His voice was loud enough to get the attention of everyone in the saloon, including Brandt, who looked up from the card game he was playing.

"Who is dead?" Brandt asked.

"Manning is dead," Pettis replied. "The fool tried to draw against Smoke Jensen."

"No," Waco said, shaking his head. "I don't believe that. He told me once that he considered drawing against another man to be playing games. And he said he would never play games."

"Yeah, well, you're partly to blame for it," Pettis said.

"Me?" Waco sputtered. "How the hell do you come up with the idea that I'm partly to blame?"

"Tell us what happened," Brandt said.

Pettis told how the two of them had split up once they got to the saloon.

"We figured we could learn more that way by each of us listenin' in to different conversations. So, Manning was standin' down to the end of the bar and I was way on the other side of the room when I heard Manning shout out for Smoke Jensen to draw." Pettis tossed the rest of his drink down, then wiped his lips with the back of his hand. "I swear, I ain't never seen nothin' as fast in my life. I mean, one moment he was standin' there, holding the barkeep's hand, and the next moment, the next breath even, his gun was in his hand and blazin' away. It was like the gun was there all along."

"What do you mean, he was holdin' the barkeep's hand?" Stone asked.

"The barkeep was shakin' hands with Smoke Jensen," Pettis explained. "And that's when Manning took his chance and draw'd down on him."

"I still don't know what the hell would make him do somethin' like that," Brandt said.

" 'Cause he figured that, what with Jensen's hand bein' busy and all, it would give him an edge. Leastwise, that's what he said just a'fore he died." Pettis glared at Waco. "And what he also said was that he done it 'cause you're always braggin' as to how you are goin' to kill Jensen. He said he figured that if he beat you to it, it would shut you up."

"Damn, he should'a known better than to try to beat Jensen, even if Jensen was holdin' someone's hand," Preston said. "Can't nobody beat Smoke Jensen, and anyone who tries is just committin' suicide."

"He can be beat," Waco said. "All it takes is the right man, and he can be beat."

"Yes, well, enough about the big, bad gunfighter and how fast he is," Brandt said. "What I want to know is, did you find out anything while you were in Benevadis? Or was your ride over there and back a total waste of time?" He stared pointedly at Pettis.

"Yeah, I found out somethin'," Pettis said. "They're braggin' and takin' on as to how they've whupped us the last two times they've run up against us. More'n once I heard one of 'em say they wish we would just come on after them so we could have us an all-out battle, like in a real war."

"Well, then, what do you say, let's go get the sons of bitches!" Waco shouted, banging his fist on the bar. "Only when we do, Smoke Jensen is mine!" He pointed his finger at everyone in the saloon. "Do all of you understand that? Smoke Jensen is mine!"

"You think you can take him, do you, Waco?" Preston asked.

"I know I can take him," Waco answered resolutely. "All it takes is skill, which I got, and guts enough not to be afraid of him."

"Waco, you are as big a fool as Manning was," Stone said. "And if you don't watch yourself, you're goin' to wind up just like him, which is deader'n shit."

Stone's observation elicited laughter from several of the others, and that made Waco angry at being the butt of the joke. He was gratified to see, however, that when he showed his anger by glaring at them, they were unable to meet his gaze.

"But Waco is partly right, ain't he, Major? We're goin' to do somethin', ain't we?" Preston asked. "I mean, I don't want to go challenge Jensen to a duel or anything like that. But it seems to me like we ought to do somethin' to kind of take the wind out of their sails before they get too big for their britches."

Brandt looked back at Pettis. "You were over there, you heard them talking. Do they have an army, like Kunz said?"

Pettis nodded. "Yes, sir, they got 'em an army all right. And they're all organized and ever'thing. From what I was able to figure out by listenin' to them talk, they've got themselves broke down into several different groups, with leaders and sharpshooters and riders and the like in each of the groups. It's like they got one big army with a lot of really little armies."

"It's called a table of organization," Brandt explained.

"So then, you figure they really did know what they was talkin' about?" Pettis asked.

Brandt nodded, and drummed his fingers on the table for a moment or two.

"Damn, imagine that. I mean, ole Captain King havin' his own private army," Preston said.

"You got 'ny thought, Major?" Stone asked.

"Yes, I've got a thought," Brandt finally said. "The way I see it, if they've got an army, that means they have declared war against us. And if they want a war, then by damn a war is what we will give them."

"Just what kind of war are you talkin' about?" Stone asked.

"The kind of war they call hell," Brandt said.

"All right," Waco said. "Let's take it to 'em. I'm gettin' tired of waitin' around."

Brandt glared at Waco again, showing his impatience with the young man's brashness. Then he turned his attention to Stone.

"Sergeant, do you remember our operation against Buffington, Missouri, back during the war?"

"Yes, sir, I remember it very well," Stone said.

"Would you say it was effective?"

Stone smiled. "Yes, sir. It was damn effective," he said.

"I've always been a strong believer in the idea that if something worked once, it will work again," Brandt said. "Gather up everything we will need."

"Yes, sir," Stone replied.

Three days later Brandt stood in front of the sheriff's office. Nearly sixty men were gathered in the street and, though they were normally raucous and out of control, they now stood quietly, awaiting his orders. That Brandt could form such miscreants into an efficient military organization spoke highly of his military skills.

During his court-martial, Brandt's defense attorney tried to point out to the judge and jurors that by incarcerating him, the Army would be losing a tactical genius.

Later, when Brandt was found guilty and sentence was passed, the judge made reference to the defense attorney's suggestion that Brandt had a brilliant military mind.

"That Major Brandt has a superb military mind is not, nor has it ever been, in dispute. The court recognizes and acknowledges his brilliance. However, rather than being an ameliorating fact, I find it disturbingly more condemning.

"A malevolent man of ordinary intelligence can do much evil. But the harm done by a man who is both brilliant and evil is incalculable. Major Brandt, you, I believe, are just such a person. And were I to assess anything less than the maximum penalty allowed me under military law, I would be guilty of malfeasance. Therefore, I sentence you to death by hanging, subject only to appeal to the commanding general of the Army."

When Brandt's case went before General Sherman for his review, he, perhaps remembering his own march through Georgia, commuted the death penalty, sentencing Brandt to fifteen years in prison.

Because Brandt's death sentence had been commuted, the prosecution didn't even try for a death sentence for Sergeant Wiley Stone, sentencing him instead to the same fifteen years' confinement that faced Brandt.

"We will ride to our objective in military formation, and we will carry out our mission with discipline and efficiency," Brandt said, addressing his men. "Now, boots in saddles. We ride out in five minutes."

It was already dark when Brandt's army rode out of Concepcion, and the staccato beat of more than sixty horses echoed by from the buildings and houses on either side of the street. By now, nearly all of the citizens had left town, even the business owners, leaving behind what goods they couldn't take with them. The few who remained stood in their dark houses now and peered around the curtains and shades as the men rode out.

At first, there was some excitement in the town, as they thought Brandt and his men were leaving for good. There were a few, though, who knew exactly what Brandt's plans were, and they shared that knowledge with the others, so that those who watched the raiders leave did so with a feeling of frustration, depression, and helplessness.

Riding at the head of the column, Brandt called his men to a halt. It was just after midnight and they had been riding for some three hours. The hill where Brandt halted them was about two hundred feet high and from there they had an excellent view of the layout of the Santa Gertrudis Ranch. To the right, as they looked down from the hill, was Casa Grande. Every window in the big house was dark, indicating that all were in bed. The two-story edifice loomed large and gleaming in the light of the full moon.

To the left of the big house was the kitchen that served the cowboys, and across from the kitchen was the bunkhouse. Then came the barn, the lot, and several other outbuildings. Finally, to the left, a full quarter of a mile away from the big house, were more than a score of small houses. Some of the houses had swings hanging from trees; others had small carts, indicating that children lived there.

"What is that town?" Preston asked, pointing to the houses.

"It isn't a real town," Brandt replied. "It's what's left of a Mex village that King moved up here so he would have workers on his ranch. They call it King's Settlement."

"Damn, it's as big as most of the towns around here."

"Who'd want to live there?" Pettis asked. "They don't have any saloons."

Some of the men laughed, but it took only one glance from Brandt to quiet them.

"Muffle all horses and equipment," Brandt ordered. "Pass it down."

"Muffle all horses and equipment."

"Muffle all horses and equipment."

The order was passed down the line until it could no longer be heard by those on the front rank.

Brandt, Stone, Waco, Preston, Pettis, and all the other riders dismounted, then tied pieces of burlap around the hooves of the horses. The horses didn't like it, and a few tried to avoid it, but soon, every hoof was wrapped. Next, the reins and harness were

wrapped as well; then, when all was prepared, Brandt gave the order to remount
and proceed at a walk.

An owl in a tree watched transfixed as the
column of men and horses passed by with
very little sound. Finding the sight of such a
large body of silently moving creatures dis-
turbing, the owl hooted, then took off, the
flapping of his wings unusually loud in the
silence of the night.

Inside one of the small houses, Rosita
Juarez was awakened by a sound that
seemed somewhat different from the regular night symphony of insects, barn animals, and distant coyotes. She lay in bed for
a moment, listening to see if she could hear
it again, but she heard nothing.

Then the baby turned over and her crib
creaked, and Rosita smiled and looked over
at her. It was the baby she'd heard.

"Duerma bien, mi Carmelita pequeño,"
she murmured.

Then, snuggling next to her husband for
warmth, she went back to sleep.

As Brandt and his riders drew closer to
the ranch and outbuildings, they could hear
the sounds of the ranch. In the stable a restless horse kicked the wall of its stall. Out in

the lot, a horse whickered. The windmill, gleaming softly in the moonlight, clanked as it answered a freshening breeze, then turned into the wind with its spinning blades scattering slivers of silver into the night.

"Spread out into a company front," Brandt said, and the riders at the rear of the column came up to either side until Brandt presented one long rank of men and horses, side by side, as they faced the ranch.

"Pass it down, right and left. Everyone but the torch men, draw weapons," Brandt ordered, still keeping his voice low.

The weapons were drawn.

"Torch men, light your torches," Brandt ordered.

Every third man in the formation lit a torch so that, soon, there were twenty blazing torches. The torches gave out a wavering orange light that brightened the night considerably.

Brandt held his sword over his head, then looked up and down the line. "Charge!" he shouted.

As one, the men and horses moved down the hill like an invading wave of fire. All attempts at silence having ended now, the horses at full gallop threw their cloth mufflings off so that the hooves thundered across the plain.

"Fire!" Brandt shouted and, concurrent with his command, forty men began firing their pistols into the houses of the little village. They swept through the houses, still unopposed, and as they passed by the buildings, the torch men threw their torches.

Almost immediately, several of the Mexican homes caught fire.

Chapter Nineteen

Sally was the one who heard it first, the sound of galloping hooves from some distance away. She'd opened her eyes wondering what it could be when she heard the first shots fired.

"Smoke!" she said, shaking him in the bed beside her. "Smoke!" she called again.

She hadn't actually needed to call him the second time. He woke when she first said his name, and even as he was waking, he heard the sound of gunfire.

Quickly, Smoke got out of bed and looked through the window of the guest bedroom. At first it was too dark to see anything, even by the light of the silver moon. Then he saw the several gleaming objects arcing through the sky. A moment later, a couple of the buildings caught fire, and in the orange glow, he could see dozens of riders, moving back and forth, firing into the houses of King's Settlement.

"It's Brandt!" Smoke said. "It has to be!"

Even as Smoke was pulling on his trousers, he heard a loud knock on his door.

"Smoke! Smoke, wake up!"

The man outside his door was Richard King. Smoke nodded at Sally, who by now had put on a robe. Sally opened the door and King was standing just outside, holding a burning candle.

"I'll be right with you," Smoke said as he pulled on his boots.

Within a matter of seconds, Smoke was running down the stairs with King just behind him. Kleberg, whose room was on the first floor, met them at the bottom of the stairs.

"Should we turn out the men?" Kleberg asked.

"Yes," Smoke said. "Tell them to get their horses saddled. I'm going to get a rifle and get up into the loft of the barn and see if I can get a shot."

"Your rifle won't be any good at that range," King said.

"Maybe not, but I'm going to try."

"Wait," King said, heading toward a walnut cabinet. "Take this." King handed Smoke a heavy rifle with a polished walnut stock and grip.

"Nice weapon," Smoke said.

"It's a Sharps Fifty," King said. "It's accurate from a mile away."

"Ammunition?"

"Here's a whole box of shells," King said, handing over a box of the large, heavy shells.

With rifle in hand, Smoke left the house, then started to spring toward the barn. Pearlie and Cal were sleeping in the bunkhouse, and they met Smoke about halfway between the house and the barn.

"Get everyone up, dressed, armed, and saddled," Smoke shouted as he ran by.

"Right," Pearlie replied, turning back toward the bunkhouse.

Smoke climbed the ladder to the barn loft, then lay down and looked through the window. By now several houses were burning, and he could hear men shouting and women screaming above the sound of the guns. He could also hear babies crying.

Smoke opened the breech of the big rifle, slid a shell in, closed the breech, then sighted down the barrel. In the light of one of the burning houses, he saw a man on a horse. The man was aiming a pistol. Smoke couldn't see the man's target, but he didn't care.

Smoke pulled the trigger. The rifle boomed and rocked back against his shoulder. An instant later he saw the pistol shooter being knocked off his horse.

Smoke ejected the smoking empty car-
tridge and put another bullet in. A moment
later he found a second target, then
squeezed the trigger. Like the first man, this
one threw up his arms and tumbled from his
saddle.

When Brandt saw the first of his men
tumble from the saddle, he thought someone might have shot him from one of the
little houses. But he heard the bullet that hit
the second man, and he knew that it came
from a long way off. Looking back toward
the shadows of the main house, he saw a
wink of flame from the muzzle blast, and an
instant later, a third of his men fell.

"Sergeant!" Brandt yelled. "Order the
withdrawal!"

"Pull back!" Stone shouted. "Pull back!"

"What the hell we pullin' back for?" one
of the men shouted. "We ain't even had a
chance at any of the women yet!"

He had no sooner gotten the words from
his mouth than he was hit in the chest by a
bullet that was so heavy that it opened up a
fist-sized hole.

Because he was protesting the pullback,
several of the others just happened to be
looking at him at the moment of impact. Realizing then that they were being picked off,

one at a time, by someone so far away that they couldn't even see him, they were on the verge of panic.

"Let's get the hell out of here!" someone shouted, and his fear spread through the others so that, like a flock of birds suddenly taking flight, everyone turned and galloped away, leaving half-a-dozen houses burning behind them.

By now Pearlie, Cal, and all the cowboys were dressed and had come to the stable to saddle their horses. In the barn, Smoke stood up and walked to the edge of the loft where he could look down at the men from the open window.

"Pearlie," he called. "Take ten men with you and follow them."

"Follow them?" Pearlie replied. "I want to do more than follow them. I want to catch the bastards."

"It's too late to catch them now. They have too much of a head start and you'll never find them in the dark. All I want you to do is make sure they don't decide to come back."

"All right, Smoke, if you say so," Pearlie said.

Smoke jumped down from the loft and threw a saddle on Stormy.

"Where are you going, Smoke?" Cal asked.

"To see what I can do to help down in the quarters," Smoke said.

The bucket brigades could do nothing for the houses that were already burning, but by wetting down the adjacent houses, they were able to prevent the fires from spreading any further. They also searched for people who had been wounded by the attack, and moved them to safety.

The fires snapped and popped as they burned and the area was bathed in a hellish, orange glow that created patches of light and dark. That created the illusion of rescue workers appearing and disappearing as they moved in and out of the light and dark.

Smoke and a few other men took a long pole and used it to collapse one burning house in on itself to prevent the fire from spreading any farther. It fell in with a roar, and the flames leapt up, but the purpose was accomplished because the fire was contained.

Standing back, Smoke wiped the back of his hand against his face, leaving a black smudge. Looking around, he saw Ramon standing with a Mexican woman. The woman was weeping almost uncontrollably.

Seeing Smoke looking toward him, Ramon came over to talk to him.

"Who is that?" Smoke asked.

Ramon looked back toward the weeping woman. "Her name is Rosita."

"Was this her house?" Smoke asked. "If so, I'm sorry we had to collapse it like that, but we had no choice."

"No, everyone understands that we had to destroy some houses to save the others," Ramon said. "Rosita's house wasn't damaged."

"Oh," Smoke said, understanding then. "She lost someone, didn't she?"

"Her baby was killed," Ramon said. "When the riders came down and started shooting up the place, a bullet went into her baby's crib."

"Oh, damn," Smoke said. He sighed and shook his head. "Oh, damn."

"Look out!" someone shouted, and Smoke looked around just as another house collapsed in on itself. The flames roared up, then sent a huge shower of sparks climbing into the sky to disappear among the stars.

"How many were killed?" Smoke asked.

"Eleven," Ramon said. "Four are women, three are children, including Rosita's baby."

"Wounded?"

"Seven, but fortunately, none of the wounds seem that severe."

King and Kleberg joined Smoke and Ramon then. Like Smoke, King's face was blackened from the smoke and burnt wood. King shook his head.

"This is awful," he said. "This is almost as bad as it was when he raided the ranch during the war. The only difference is, I wasn't here then, and I told myself that it could never have happened if I had been here." King sighed and pinched the bridge of his nose. "Well, I am here now," he said. "And it didn't make any difference. It didn't make one damn bit of difference. Brandt came in here and burned the houses and killed women and children, and there wasn't a thing I could do about it."

"How many people got put out of their homes?" Smoke asked.

"I'm not sure," King answered. "Bob, a count."

"Seven houses were completely destroyed, four were so badly damaged that people can't live in them now, and three more were partially damaged," Kleberg said.

"Ramon, tell your people that we will rebuild the houses right away," King said, quickly. "And we'll repair the ones that need it."

"My people know that, Captain King," Ramon replied. "They are sorry that this trouble has fallen on you."

"On us, my friend," King said, putting his hand on Ramon's shoulder. "It has fallen on us."

"Where will the people stay until the houses are rebuilt?" Smoke asked.

"Do not worry about that, Señor Smoke," Ramon replied. "We are all friends and family here. We will make room for those who lost their homes. And if there isn't room for everyone, Padre Bustamante will make room for them in the church."

"Pearlie, they are heading toward the Santa Gertrudis," Barrett said. "They probably think there is only one ford, and that's the one some miles west of here. But I know another one that's a lot closer. If we go this way" — he pointed to the southeast — "I think we can beat them across and be waiting on the other side."

"Wait a minute," Spitz said. "Are you talkin' about the Garza ford?"

"Yes," Barrett said.

"That's a bar that's no more'n four feet wide. That's not a place to cross in the dark."

"I know it ain't," Barrett said. "That's

why I know they're goin' to go all the way to the other ford to get across."

"Can you get us across this Garza ford in the middle of the night?" Pearlie asked.

"Yes."

"There's another thing you might want to think about," Spitz said. "I mean, I don't know if you boys seen the raiders as well as I did, but there was at least forty or fifty in that bunch, maybe more. And if you look around, there's only ten of us."

"Do you think they would expect us to beat them across the river and be waiting for them?" Pearlie asked.

Spitz shook his head. "I doubt they even know about the Garza ford. No, I'm sure they won't be expecting us."

"Then we'll just hide and wait for them as they cross," Pearlie said. "We won't attack them head-on, but I do intend to get a few licks in. Lead the way, Barrett."

Riding hard, Pearlie, Barrett, Spitz, and the others reached the Santa Gertrudis. Then, with Barrett leading the way, they crossed the ford in single file.

Once on the other side, they rode quickly down the river until they reached the Duval ford, which was wide enough to drive entire herds of cattle across.

"You and you, stay back here and hold our

266

horses," Pearlie said, choosing two men that he knew were not among the best shots.

"What the hell, and miss out on the fun?" one of the men asked.

"Don't gripe about it, Billy, they do it this way in the Army," Barrett said. "When the cavalry fights dismounted, one in four holds the horses."

"Yeah," Billy said. "But why me?"

" 'Cause you can't hit a bull in the ass from forty paces," Spitz said, and the others laughed.

"Come on, let's get in position," Pearlie ordered, and the men ran, crouched over, along the bank of the stream until they found places that provided both cover and concealment.

They waited for almost an hour, so long that they were losing the cover of darkness, but still, they had seen no one. The sun was not yet up, but it had grown much lighter in the east, and distant objects began to come into view. Pearlie was beginning to wonder if Brandt's men had managed to cross the stream ahead of them, and was about to call the whole thing off when they heard the sound of hoofbeats.

"Get ready!" Pearlie called to his men. "Fire when I fire."

It was now light enough for Pearlie to see

what they were up against, and he gasped at the size of the army. There were at least sixty, maybe more, and they hit the stream at a gallop, churning up the water so that a fountain of bubbles was sustained as they came across.

At first, Pearlie was going to fire while they were in the river, but at the last moment he held back, reasoning that if he took them on head-on, they would have no choice but to come after their attackers. So, Pearlie waited until they were across and started down the road before he opened fire.

Immediately after he fired the first shot, the others in his group started shooting. He had the satisfaction of seeing three men fall from their saddles, and a fourth grab his arm.

Riding at the head of the column, Brandt didn't even realize immediately that they were under fire. When he did discover it, he had no idea how many there were, so he reacted as any military leader would when caught in an ambush. He moved his men quickly through the killing grounds. Standing in his stirrups, he shouted the order back to his men.

"Forward at a gallop!"

The raiders broke into a gallop, riding away quickly, paying no heed whatever to the men they were leaving behind.

After Brandt was gone, Pearlie and the others moved out to examine the men who were lying on the ground. "I need one of them alive," he said to the others. "I want to question him."

"Pearlie, this one is still alive," Spitz called from one of the bodies.

Pearlie hurried over to him, then looked down at the wounded man.

"What is your name?" Pearlie asked.

"Why should I give you my name?" the man answered.

"Because we're about to bury you," Pearlie replied. "Don't you want your friends and family to know where you are?"

"I ain't got no friends or family," the man said. He chuckled. "And if nobody knows where I am, maybe the devil won't be able to find me." He tried to laugh at his own joke, but it turned into a couple of wheezing coughs; then he died.

"What now?" Barrett asked.

"We'll bury them," Pearlie said. "Then we'll get back to the ranch and see what we can do to help out."

"Major, those men who attacked us," Stone said. "Where the hell did they come from?"

"It would seem that they had a wandering scout out for just such an occasion," Brandt said. "That's pretty smart of Mr. Jensen. I won't be underestimating him again."

Chapter Twenty

As the sun rose on King's Settlement, a pall of smoke lay over the burned-out shells of what had once been houses. Those who were burned out, as well as the luckier residents of the little settlement whose houses had not been destroyed, were picking through the twisted and blackened rubble to see what they could salvage.

"La fotografía de mi madre! Ella sobrevivir!" one woman cried happily as she pulled a photograph out of the ashes. As she had stated, her mother's picture had survived.

The morning air was permeated with the aroma of coffee, bacon, biscuits, and eggs, because the ranch cook had brought up the chuck wagon and prepared breakfast for everyone. Sally contributed freshly made doughnuts she had made back at the main house, and here and there could be seen a cowboy, or an entire family, eating their breakfast from tin plates.

Pearlie and the others returned from their

sortie just as breakfast was being served and, with a broad smile, Cal pointed out that fact to him.

"Pearlie, you don't ever need to buy yourself a pocket watch," Cal said. "You always know when it's mealtime."

"I was just lucky," Pearlie said. He didn't go to the chuck wagon, but grabbed a couple of the doughnuts and a cup of coffee instead. There was a line waiting for breakfast, and despite his known chowhound tendencies, Pearlie was hanging back until all the men who had ridden out with him were fed.

"What did you see?" Smoke asked.

"A lot of men," Pearlie said around a bite of doughnut. "A hell of a lot of men. Fifty, sixty, maybe more."

"So you did catch up with them?" Cal asked.

"Yes, thanks to Barrett," Pearlie said. He dunked the doughnut in his coffee, then took another bite. "Barrett knew another ford across the Santa Gertrudis. We took that, got across before they did, then waited for them, and hit them when they came across."

"What? You attacked sixty men with ten?" Smoke asked. "Pearlie, that's a dumb thing to do. It's a wonder you are still alive."

"I didn't attack them head-on," Pearlie replied, a little stung by Smoke's remark. "I waited until they passed before I attacked. That way, they had no idea how many of us there were, so they skedaddled. Ha! You should have seen them run."

Smoke realized that his reprimand had hurt Pearlie's feelings, and he ameliorated his remark by reaching out to squeeze Pearlie's shoulder.

"I'm sorry about the sharpness of tone," he apologized. "But I was worried about you. I should have known better. You did it just right, and I'm proud of you."

Now, under Smoke's praise, Pearlie beamed. "Thanks," he said. "I just asked myself, what would Smoke do, and I did it."

"So, did you get any of them?" Cal asked.

"Yes," Pearlie replied. "We killed three, and we wounded at least one."

"Good!" Cal said. "By damn, we made the sons of bitches pay for what they did here."

"Not enough," Smoke replied. "Even counting the four that were killed here, that still leaves us with four more dead than they had. And six more wounded."

Pearlie was about to take another bite of his second doughnut when he heard that, and he paused.

"You mean we had eleven killed?"

"Yes," Smoke said.

Pearlie shook his head. "Damn."

"And that's not the worst of it," Cal put it. "Most of the dead are women and kids, including one baby."

Pearlie was quiet for a long moment.

"You all right?" Smoke asked.

"Yeah," Pearlie said. He sighed. "Listen, Smoke, we've got to find that son of a bitch and kill him. I mean, this has nothing to do with you doing a favor for a friend now, or anything like that. This has become personal."

"How has it become personal?" Cal asked. "You don't know any of the people who were killed."

"It's personal for me," Pearlie said.

"Yeah," Smoke said, looking out at the faces of the people of King's Settlement as they went about the business of trying to pick up the pieces of their lives. "It's that way for me too."

Once again, a mass funeral was held at King's Settlement. Places were reserved in the little church for Smoke, Sally, Pearlie, and Cal, but they declined, saying it was more important that those who actually knew the deceased be able to attend.

After the service inside, everyone moved

out to the cemetery, where Smoke and the others who had not found room in the church joined the mourners. Eleven new graves were added to the cemetery. The still-fresh mounds of the most recent victims of Major Jack Brandt were prominent by their newness.

The most poignant of all the graveside rites was the one for the burial of little Carmelita Juarez. Rosita was not the only one to shed tears over this burial. There were very few dry eyes in the gathering as the small coffin was lowered into the ground.

Afterward, as the mourners returned to their homes, Smoke, Sally, Pearlie, and Cal joined Captain Richard and Henrietta King, Alice King, and Bob Kleberg for dinner at the big house.

"Smoke," Kleberg said over the dinner table. "Richard and I have been talking."

"Oh?"

"This has turned out to be a lot more than you bargained for," Kleberg said. "I know it is more than we bargained for. So, if you want to get on the train and go back to Colorado, I want you to know that we would understand."

"Could you pass the mashed potatoes, please?" Smoke asked Alice, who was sitting in front of them.

"Of course," Alice said.

Smoke spooned a second helping of mashed potatoes onto his plate before he answered.

"Are you afraid that we are eating you out of house and home, Captain King?" Smoke asked with a smile. "If so, that is a legitimate worry. You certainly do set a fine table."

"I'll say," Pearlie said as he helped himself to some more peas.

"And, as you can see by Pearlie's appetite, you know now why I suggested that he and Cal bunk and eat with the cowboys."

"If you ask me, Smoke, you had us bunk out there so you could keep all this good food to yourself," Pearlie said as he grabbed two more biscuits. "Oh, not that food out there isn't good," he added quickly. "I don't want you to think I don't enjoy it or any-thing."

"Mr. Jensen, did you ask me if I'm afraid you are eating me out of house and home? No, no, of course not," King sputtered. "Why would you ask such a thing? Why would you even think such a thing?"

"I was just wondering why you were trying to get rid of us, that's all," Smoke said.

"Smoke," Sally said, scolding him. Then she smiled at King. "Captain King, I think what my husband is trying to tell you, in his very clumsy way" — she looked back at Smoke with a scowl on her face — "is that he is more than willing to stay and see this through with you. In fact, after the events of the last few days, I think he is more determined than ever."

"Damn right," Pearlie said resolutely. Then, quickly, he put his hand over his lips.

"Excuse me, Mrs. King, Miss Alice, and Miss Sally," Pearlie said. "I didn't mean to be profane and go swearing like that."

Henrietta laughed. "Young man, don't you worry about a thing," she said. "Just knowing that you are willing to stay and help us is all we need."

"Thank you, ma'am. Uh, do we have any dessert?"

Because Brandt's men tended to stay up all night drinking, or pursuing other forms of nocturnal entertainment, they slept through most of the day. Shortly after they arrived in town, they took over the hotel, without offering any compensation to the owner, sometimes crowding from six to eight into a single room. But as citizens of the town began leaving town, Brandt's men started moving into the houses the fleeing townspeople had abandoned.

The mayor of the town, Julio Hernandez, watched with great dismay as the citizens of his town kept leaving. At the rate they were going, Concepcion would be a ghost town within another few days.

Of course, he thought, it might be better off as a ghost town. Anything would be better than what was happening now, with this army of outlaws taking over everything.

It was mid-afternoon, and Julio was standing at the front door of his office, looking out, when he saw three of the citizens of the town coming toward his office. Tad Beeker, the owner of the hotel, was the only American in the group.

"Mr. Mayor," Beeker said. "If you don't mind, we would like a word with you."

"All right," Julio said, not sure what the visit was about.

"Something has to be done," Beeker said.

"Something has to be done? *No comprendo.*"

"Well, let me put it in plain English for you, Señor Hernandez," Beeker said in an exasperated tone of voice. "We want something done about Brandt and his men."

"What would you have me do?"

"Well, for starters, you could present him with a bill," Beeker said. "It's bad enough that they ran all my paying customers off. They aren't paying to stay in the hotel."

"I am the mayor of the town, Señor Beeker. I am not a bill collector."

"But you also represent the law. And the law says that a businessman who is charging a fair price has to be paid. Otherwise, it's the same as stealin'."

"Are you feeding them? Are you keeping the rooms and the bed clothing clean?" Julio asked.

"Hell, no, I'm not," Beeker said angrily. "Not for those sons of bitches." He pointed toward the hotel.

"What about you two?" Julio asked. "Do you also have a *queja?* A complaint?"

"*Sí,*" Manuel said. "Many have now moved out of the hotel and are staying in houses. Some are staying in my sister's house."

"Yes," Julio said. "Well, that is the fault of your sister. She is the one who left. If we had all stuck together in the beginning . . ."

"We would have all been killed together," Manuel said.

Julio paused for a moment, then nodded. "I think you are right," he said. "Which brings me back to my question. You are here complaining to me about it. What do you expect me to do?"

"Run them out," Beeker said.

"And how should I do that?"

"I don't know. Pass an ordinance or something. Issue a proclamation. Do whatever it takes, just run them out of town."

"If you want someone run out of town, Mr. Beeker, I suggest you come to me," a new voice suddenly said. "As your sheriff, that is my job."

Beeker felt his blood run cold and, nervously, he turned to see Brandt standing just inside the door.

"Come to you?" Beeker said. His voice was subdued.

"Yes, come to me. I want to run a good town here. I want to keep order, so, if you are having a problem, just come to me."

"I . . . uh . . . am having no problem," Beeker mumbled. "Mr. Mayor, I have to go," he said, starting toward the door.

"I do too," Manuel said.

"Me too," the third visitor said.

Within seconds after Brandt had entered the room, everyone else had departed.

"Well, now," Brandt said, laughing as he watched them leave. "Did I step in some sheep shit or something? What do you think made them all run off like that?"

"I think they just had business to tend to," Julio said nervously.

"What could possibly be more important business than keeping order in our town? And you have to admit, outside of that unfortunate incident when one of the citizens of your town was accidentally killed . . ."

"Accidentally?" Julio replied. "Tomas was shot right between the eyes!"

"Yes, but my man wasn't aiming to hit him between the eyes. He wanted to shoot off his hat. Surely, you can see that he didn't do it on purpose."

"But, Señor, surely you can see how trying to shoot off a man's hat is not the thing a man should be doing. It is loco."

"I agree," Brandt said. "That's why I have punished the guilty person. He cannot come back to the saloon. If I see him there, I will put him in jail and this I promise you. Now, what else is bothering you?"

Julio sighed. "Nothing, Señor," he said. "Nothng is bothering me."

Brandt sighed. "I didn't think so. Listen, Mayor, you don't mind if we use your office for a while, do you? I have some meetings planned, and the sheriff's office just isn't set up for what I need to do."

Julio wanted to protest, but knew that it would be senseless to do so. Instead, he merely shrugged his shoulders.

"Mi casa es su casa," he said quietly.

"I knew you would understand," Brandt said. "Now, if you would, please go somewhere. My men and I have military strategy to discuss."

Angry at being run out of his own office, and frustrated because he could do nothing about it, Julio swallowed his pride and left.

Within minutes after Julio left, Stone came into the office, followed somewhat later by Preston and Waco. Pettis came in shortly afterward.

"Men, I thank you for coming," Brandt said.

"Major, are you the mayor now?" Pettis asked.

"No, I'm perfectly content to be the sheriff, and your commanding officer," Brandt replied. "And that brings me to the purpose of this meeting. As you know, from the beginning, I have run this outfit like a military outfit. I believe that my military experience can serve us well in accomplishing our objective. Until now, I have had only Sergeant Stone to help me, but I am today appointing each of you to the rank of corporal."

The three men looked at each other and smiled.

"Does that mean the other men have got to say sir to us?" Preston asked.

"You only say sir to officers," Stone pointed out.

"Sergeant Stone is correct," Brandt said. He held up his finger to make a point. "But each of you will have a great deal of responsibility, for I intend to break our battalion down into four companies and each of you will be in charge of a company."

"Well now, how about that?" Pettis asked. "Me in charge of a company."

"Secondly, I want to congratulate each of you — and I want you to pass those congratulations on to your men — as to how you performed your duty the other night during our raid against Captain King's ranch. You carried out your orders without question and, as a result, the mission was a success."

"Yeah, but what good was it?" Preston asked.

"What *good* was it?" Brandt repeated. "What do you mean, what good was it? Weren't you there?"

"Well, yes, sir, I was there, all right, shootin' and screamin' and burnin' with the rest of 'em," Preston replied. "But I mean, other than burning some houses, and maybe killing a few people, what did we do? What was it all about? Because it sure wasn't about money."

"Are you questioning the major, Preston?"

Stone asked sternly. "If so, maybe we better get another corporal."

"Don't get me wrong, I ain't exactly questionin' the major. It's just that, well, when we all joined up with this army, we was told we would be getting a lot of money. We ain't seen any of that money yet, and I was just wonderin' when we would, that's all."

"Corporal Preston, may I suggest that you leave the planning to me?" Brandt said.

"Yes, sir," Preston replied. "I didn't mean nothin' by it. Like I say, I was just wonderin' when we was goin' to see some money. That's all."

"Well, you can quit wondering because I'm going to tell you," Brandt said. "I'm going to tell all of you," he added, taking in the other corporals at the meeting.

"What we are doing is pure military strategy. We are conducting raids to undermine the morale and courage of King's men. We killed several of them during our raid the other night. And it is my guess that several of King's workers will now be leaving the Santa Gertrudis. Before long, Captain King will have so few people left to work his cattle that when he starts his drive north, he will be so shorthanded that he can barely control the herd."

Brandt smiled broadly, and brought his

hand down pointedly. "And that, my friends, is when we will move in, take his herd, and continue to Kansas with it. We'll sell the herd, we'll be rich, and Captain Richard King will be as poor as a church mouse."

"How does that sound to you boys?" Stone asked.

"Sounds damn good to me," Preston said.

"After we sell the herd, we'll split up the money and be on our separate ways," Brandt said.

"How does this here split work?" Pettis asked.

"Obviously, as leaders, we will get the larger share," he said. "I will get one third of the total, Sergeant Stone will get one third of what is left, you boys will divide up one third of what remains after the sergeant and I have taken our cut. The rest of the money will be divided evenly among the men. As you can see, being a noncommissioned officer pays well in my army."

"That sounds good to me," Preston said with a wide, satisfied smile on his face.

"When do I get to kill Smoke Jensen?" Waco asked.

Brandt looked at Waco. "Just wait, my young, impatient friend. Trust me. You will get your opportunity to test your fast-draw and shooting skills against the legendary Smoke Jensen."

"There ain't no test to it," Waco said. "I'll beat the son of a bitch. I can guarantee you that."

"I'll pay to watch that, Waco," Pettis said.

"I will too," Stone added.

"Now, men, let's get on with our meeting," Brandt said. He cleared his throat. "Although you men performed your duty well last night, I was a failure."

"What? How do you get that, Major?" Stone asked. "I thought you done a real good job, plannin' it and all."

Brandt shook his head. "I underestimated my enemy," he said. "That's one of the biggest mistakes a commander can make. I did not plan on anyone sitting off a quarter of a mile or farther and being able to pick us off at will. But that is just what happened during our raid. Someone, and I suspect it was Smoke Jensen, was up in the loft of the barn, shooting us with a heavy-caliber rifle. He had us ranged, and the rifle fire was deadly accurate. Then, as we withdrew, he had an ambush set up at the river crossing."

"Yeah," Pettis said. "We lost some more men there too."

"Indeed we did, and I let both things happen because I did not take Smoke

Jensen, or his military skills, into consideration when I planned the attack."

"Hell, Major, we don't none of us blame you none," Preston said.

"We are going to conduct some more military operations against Captain King's ranch, and against the army this man Smoke Jensen has created," Brandt said. He turned to the map of Duval County that was on the wall behind the mayor's desk. "Only this time, I intend to plan more carefully," he said as he pointed to the map.

"I intend to divide Captain King's ranch into three sections. Each of you will be responsible for one section."

He drew a huge Y across the map, then assigned each of the new "corporals" a wedge. "I will hold you personally responsible for everything that happens within your area of responsibility. Also, I will expect you to begin a campaign of harassment and interdiction."

"Harassment and what?" Waco asked.

"Harassment and interdiction," Brandt repeated. "You will find cowboys working in your area, and you will kill them."

Chapter Twenty-one

Pettis, Waco, and Preston began Brandt's operation of harassment and interdiction that very night. Sending their men out alone, or in pairs, they rode the range, looking for isolated cowboys.

Waco was the first one to strike. Lying in wait behind a clump of bushes, he watched a lone rider coming toward him. When the cowboy was even with him, he stood up, startling the rider with his sudden and unexpected appearance.

"Madre de Dios. Quién es usted?" the rider asked. "Who are you?"

"I am an Angel *del diablo,*" Waco said with an evil chuckle as he pulled the trigger.

Three of Captain King's men were killed on the first day of the harassment and interdiction operation, and two more over the next three days and nights.

Each day Brandt would send his companies out to ride the range, looking for targets of opportunity.

"Do this enough times, and King won't

have anyone left working for him," Brandt said.

"King must have two hundred men working for him," Pettis said. "Maybe more. We ain't goin' to be able to kill two hundred men one at a time."

"We don't have to kill two hundred," Brandt said. "That's the beauty of it, don't you see? If we kill enough, it will get to the point that for every one man we kill, ten will leave. We are conducting a fear and terror campaign. Remember, all we have to do is strike terror into the hearts of his cowboys, and they will be too frightened to work for him."

"Terror riders," Waco said. "Yeah, I like that."

Emilio worked in the kitchen on the Santa Gertrudis Ranch. He was returning from Corpus Christi with a load of groceries, a trip that he made at least twice a month. The trip took two days, but he didn't mind it at all. In fact, he rather enjoyed the solitude, and driving the wagon wasn't as hard as the work the cook gave him to do when he was back on the ranch. He had actually approached the cook with the idea of letting him make immediate turnaround trips, rather than waiting until supplies were needed.

"I can't spare you as a full-time grocery boy," the cook replied. "There are too many times when I need you here."

Emilio was fairly certain that would be the answer, but he figured that it wouldn't hurt to try.

The wagon was old and the wood sun-dried, which made it give off a rather pungent smell. He didn't mind the smell; it was so much a part of his life and routine that he found the aroma comfortable, like the smell of flour on his mother's apron when he was a boy.

Emilio drove the wagon along the rutted road, Captain King's private road now, because he was actually on ranch property and had been for most of the day. As the wagon rolled along, negotiating the ruts and holes, Emilio began singing. He had been thinking about buying a mouth organ. He had never played one, but he was pretty sure that he could play it if he had one.

When the sun set that night, Emilio un-hitched and hobbled his team, then had his supper of beans, tortillas, and coffee. Afterward, with a piece of canvas and a blanket, he made his bed under the wagon. That done, he stretched out under the wagon and went to sleep.

Preston had seen the wagon just before

sundown and, trailing it, stayed just out of sight until the wagon stopped. He watched the driver disconnect his team, eat his supper, then make a bedroll under the wagon. All this time, the driver was well within rifle range, and Preston could have shot him quite easily. But if his job really was to spread terror, he knew that there were more frightening ways to die. He waited until the driver was asleep.

Ramon was having a second cup of coffee when the cook came over to talk to him.

"Ramon, I am concerned about Emilio. He should have returned with the groceries yesterday. He has been late before, but he has never been this late."

"Would you like me to look for him?" Ramon asked.

"Yes. I'm afraid that the old wagon he was driving may have broken down. And if that is so, then Emilio is just conscientious enough to stay with it until someone comes rather than leave the groceries unguarded."

"I'll have a look," Ramon promised.

It was late afternoon when Ramon saw a sight that sent chills through him. Buzzards were circling around something on the ground and, whatever it was, it was big enough to have attracted several dozen of the scavengers.

Ramon quickened his pace and closed the distance between him and the buzzards quickly. That's when he saw what was drawing their attention.

Even from there, he could tell that Emilio was dead. He was sitting on the ground alongside the wagon, his right arm stretched out toward and tied to the front wheel, his left arm stretched out toward and tied to the back wheel. He was naked, and his stomach had been cut open so that his entrails were spilled onto the ground.

The wagon was empty, having been looted by Emilio's killers. The team of horses was still hobbled, unaffected by the gruesome sight, and because they were within easy range of both food and water, they had made no effort to wander off.

Ramon wrapped Emilio's body in canvas, and put him in the wagon. Then, with his own horse tied onto the wagon, Ramon drove the rig back to the main house.

Emilio was the third to die in as many days, and the cumulative effect of seeing their friends and coworkers being killed so indiscriminately was having its effect on the other workers at the ranch. As Brandt had predicted, several of the employees at Santa Gertrudis quit.

Ramon could always tell when one of them was coming to him to tender his resignation. He would appear in front of Ramon, holding his hat in his hands, looking down at the ground, while behind him his wife and children would stand waiting.

"You are a good man, Roberto," Ramon told one of them. "I hate to see you leave."

"I would not leave, Señor Ramon, if it weren't for my wife. She is afraid that something bad will happen to me."

"What bad can happen to you, Roberto? You are a carpenter. You have nothing to do with the cattle."

"Neither did Emilio. He was but a helper in the kitchen, but he was killed," Roberto pointed out.

"Señor King, I am sorry to say that many of our people are leaving," Ramon told King a couple of days later.

"Why?" King asked.

"I think it was bad enough when some of the riders were killed," Ramon said. "But Emilio worked in the kitchen. He was but a cook's helper. Why was he killed? I think many are disturbed by this."

"Of course they are upset," King said.

"They have every right to be upset. I am upset by this as well. But don't you see? This is exactly what Brandt wants. He wants to spread terror among our people. He wants you to quit. And if you do that, you are letting him dictate what you do with your own lives. Do that, and he wins."

"I have told the people this," Ramon said.

"And what do they say?"

"I am sorry, Señor King. But it has not changed their minds. Many are still leaving. And it is getting very difficult to find someone who will ride nighthawk. They are afraid they will be killed like Emilio, like the others."

King stroked his jaw for a moment, then he nodded. "All right, I can't blame them," he finally said. "Tell those who will continue to work for me, and agree to ride nighthawk, that I will double their salary. Tell those who leave that I wish them the very best."

"I will tell them, Señor," Ramon said. "Señor King . . . ? he began, then stopped in mid-sentence.

"Yes?"

"I believe that if I had something else to tell them, if I could tell them that we are fighting back and that we will win, perhaps more would stay."

"We will fight back. We are fighting back," King said.

"But how, Señor? How do you fight against such evil?" Ramon asked. "When someone wishes to spread terror, there is nothing you can do to stop them."

"Sure there is," Smoke said. "We can give terror right back to them."

"I don't know what you have in mind, Smoke," King said. "But whatever it is, you've got my support."

"We will fight back by using their own tactics against them," Smoke said. "They are killing our people, we will kill theirs."

"But how? All of our cowboys are armed now," King said. "And yet, still they get killed."

"We just have to be a little better at it, that's all," Smoke said.

Smoke went on his own personal hunting trip, not for game, but for men. He did this by using himself for bait, riding nighthawk, pretending to be so involved with his duty that he was paying no attention to what was going on around him. He had been out on the range for four days and nights now, but had not yet drawn any attention. On the fifth night out, tired of jerky, he killed a rabbit and

295

spitted it over an open flame to cook for his supper.

It was during supper that he struck pay dirt, for he realized that he was being watched. Slowly, and showing no sign that he even knew that anyone was out there, he extinguished the fire and spread out his bedroll as if he were about to go to bed. He was careful to place his boots at the foot of the bedroll, and his hat at the top. After that he crawled down into the blanket, lay there for a moment, then, in the darkness, silently rolled away and slid down into a small gully that ran nearby. Pulling his pistol, he cocked it as quietly as he could and inched back up to the top of the gully to stare through the darkness toward the bedroll.

From there, with his boots and hat in position, it looked exactly as if someone were in the blankets, sound asleep. Smoke smiled in grim approval. If his campsite looked that way to him, it would look that way to whoever was watching him.

He waited.

Out on the prairie a coyote howled.

An owl hooted.

A falling star flashed across the dark soft sky. An evening breeze moaned through the mesquite.

And still he waited.

Almost a full hour after Smoke had "gone to bed," the night was lit up by the great flame pattern produced by the discharge of a shotgun. The roar of the shotgun boomed loudly, and Smoke saw dust and bits of cloth fly up from his bedroll where a charge of buckshot tore into it. Had he been there, the shot's impact debris would have been bone and flesh rather than dust and cloth, and he would be a dead man.

Instantly thereafter, Smoke snapped a shot off toward the muzzle flash, though he was just guessing that that was where his adversary was, as he had no real target.

"Oh, you sonofabitch! You're a smart one, you are," a voice shouted almost jovially. The voice was not near the muzzle flash, and Smoke knew that his would-be assailant must have fired and moved. Whoever this was, he was no amateur. Even as Smoke thought this, he realized that the assailant could use the flame pattern from his own pistol as a target, so he threw himself to the right, just as the shotgun roared a second time. Though none of the pellets hit him, they dug into the earth where he had been but an instant earlier and sent a spray of stinging sand into his face. Smoke fired again, again aiming at the muzzle blast, though by now he knew there would be no one there. A moment later he heard the sound of retreating hoofbeats and he knew that his attacker was riding away.

As Wiley Stone rode away, he realized that his target had not been an ordinary cowboy. Whoever it was, was smart enough to fool him into thinking he was still in his bedroll. That might be a cautious cowboy's way of protecting himself, but Stone was startled by the suddenness with which his fire was returned.

Damn! Stone suddenly realized that the cowboy wasn't just protecting himself. He had set himself up as bait! He wanted to be shot at!

Stone hurried back to Concepcion to give his report to Brandt.

"Are you sure it was Smoke Jensen?" Brandt asked.

"Well, no, there was no way of tellin', it bein' night 'n all," Stone said. "But whoever it was, was some smart son of a bitch, I'll say that."

Pearlie and Cal followed Smoke's lead, going out at night and offering themselves for bait. Cal killed one his first night out. Pearlie got started late, but he got two over the next three nights. Smoke also got two so that among them, they killed five of Brandt's men.

"This ain't workin', Major," Stone said as they began appraising their losses. "They're killin' more of us now than we're killin' of them."

"Yes," Brandt said, stroking his chin. "The battle of attrition does seem to be running against us. It is obvious we are going to have to try another tactic."

"Yeah, well, what sort of other tactic do you have in mind?"

"Superior numbers," Brandt said. "From now on, we will not engage the enemy until we know that we have more people than he does."

Even as Brandt and his men were lamenting their losses, the Santa Gertrudis riders were celebrating their victories.

"I don't mind tellin' you boys, I was planning on hightailing it out of here," Barrett said. "But the way ole Smoke and the other two boys has been cuttin' down the rustlers, I don't figure there's enough of 'em left to give us any more trouble. And that's good, because we've got us a lot more cows to bring in before the drive starts."

"I think I will talk to everyone again," Ramon said. "I think now they will stay." He smiled at Barrett. "How many will you need to bring up the half-meadow herd?"

"I won't need no more'n five, I don't reckon," Barrett said.

"I will get five men for you."

"I will be one of the five," Cal offered. He looked at Pearlie. "What about you?"

"Sure, I'll go," Pearlie said. "Say, Smoke, do you think we could talk Miss Sally into cookin' us up a bunch of bear claws to take along?"

"Why don't you ask me?" Sally asked, coming up at that moment.

"Oh, uh, I didn't see you," Pearlie said. "But how about it? Would you make us up a batch?"

Sally smiled. "I think that could be arranged."

"Maybe a double batch," Pearlie said.

"A double batch?"

"Well, we are goin' to be out there for quite a while," Pearlie said. "And a man can get awful hungry out on the range."

Sally chuckled. "All right, I'll fix you a double batch," she said.

"And maybe some fried apple pies?" Pearlie suggested.

"You are impossible, Pearlie," Sally said.

"Talk about the camel getting his nose under the tent. My advice to you is, don't force it."

"Yes, ma'am," Pearlie said quickly, realizing that he had come close to overstepping himself.

Chapter Twenty-two

Pearlie was bent low over his mount's neck. The horse's mane and tail were streaming out behind, and its nostrils flared wide as it worked the powerful muscles in its shoulders and haunches. Cal was riding just behind Pearlie, urging his animal to keep pace, and Barrett was riding beside him. Behind Pearlie, Cal, and Barrett rode three more cowboys.

The six men hit a shallow creek in full stride, and sand and silver bubbles flew up in a sheet of spray, sustained by the churning action of the horses' hooves until huge drops began falling back like rain. Pearlie led the men toward an island in the middle of the stream.

"We'll hold here!" Pearlie shouted.

Dismounting, the six men took up positions where they could use shrubbery and the slight elevation of land to provide both concealment and cover. They had been peacefully pushing a small herd of cows back to join the roundup, when they were put to flight by the sudden appearance of forty riders.

Because there had been so few rustlers seen on the Santa Gertrudis Ranch over the last few days, the men had grown complacent, thinking that the worst was over. The unexpected appearance of so many men, all firing weapons as they came swooping down over a little rise of land, caused Pearlie and the others to make a desperate dash back to a small island in the middle of the stream.

"How many are there?" Barrett asked. "Did anyone get a count?"

"Too many to fight off!" Cal answered.

"Yeah, well, too many or not, we're going to have to fight them off, so we'd better get ready," Pearlie said. "We'll be making our stand here."

"We can't stay here! We got to skedaddle!" one of the cowboys said.

"Have you got any idea just where we might run to?" Pearlie asked. "We were running as hard as we could just to get here."

"Maybe if we surrender," the cowboy suggested.

"Surrender and do what? Get our carcasses spread-eagled with our guts cut out? You do remember what happened to Emilio, don't you?"

"Yeah," the cowboy responded grimly.

"Yeah, you're right. We ain't got no choice but to fight."

Pearlie was glad to see that the cowboy's near panic had been replaced by a quiet determination.

"Damn right," Pearlie said. "They may kill us, but we're goin' to kill one hell of a lot of them first."

Pearlie pointed to the neck of the island, which faced the eastern bank of the creek, the direction from which they had just come.

"I think our best bet is to try and squirm down through the tall grass. We'll take positions as near to the point as we can get, and do as much damage as we can when they start across the water."

"What do you think, Pearlie? Do you think we can stop them?" Barrett asked.

"We'll know the answer to that in about two minutes," Pearlie said. "Now, hurry, get into position. And try and stay out of sight. I'm going to take this log. Barrett, you take that tree; Pedro, that stump; Julio, you and Billy go over there behind that rock."

As the men hurried to take up their positions, Pearlie shouted more instructions. "Hold your fire until the last possible moment. Then make your shots count!"

"Pearlie, you didn't say where you wanted me," Cal said.

"I want you to go for help."

"What?"

"You are the best rider here. I want you to get back to the ranch. Tell Smoke where we are. Tell him to get here as fast as he can. If he gets here soon enough, some of us may still be alive."

"No, Pearlie, don't make me do this!" Cal protested. "I don't aim to show my tail while the rest of you are stayin' here to face them."

"Oh, for God's sake, Cal, do it!" Barrett said. "Do you think any of us would actually think you are running?"

"Don't you understand, Cal? If you don't go for help, none of us are going to get out of this alive!" Pearlie said. "You are our only chance."

"All right," Cal agreed. "I guess if you put it like that, I've got no choice." He put his foot into the stirrup, then swung up into the saddle.

"Good luck!" Pearlie shouted, slapping Cal's horse on the rump. The others shouted as well as Cal hit the water on the west side of the island, away from where the main body of their pursuers were. Pearlie watched Cal gallop north along the west bank of the creek until the horse crested an embankment. Then Pearlie turned back to await the rustlers.

"Here they come!" Barrett said. His announcement wasn't necessary, however, for by then everyone could hear the drumming of the hoofbeats as well as the cries of the rustlers themselves, yipping and barking and screaming at the top of their lungs.

The rustlers crested the bluff just before the creek; then, without a pause, they rushed down the hill toward the water, their horses sounding like thunder.

"Remember, boys, hold your fire!" Pearlie shouted. "Hold your fire until I give you the word!"

The attackers rushed into the water, riding hard across the fifty-yard-wide shallows. Then three of them pulled ahead of the others, and when they were halfway across the water, Pearlie gave the order to fire. All three of the outlaws went down.

Although there were only five defenders on the island, their fire was so effective that the outlaws who remained swerved to the right and left, riding by, rather than over, the cowboys' positions.

The outlaws regrouped on the west bank, then turned and rode back for a second charge. Again, the defenders' fire was so effective that the outlaws separated as they approached the island, like a swiftly flowing river parting around a rock.

"Is anyone hit?" Pearlie called to the others.

All four answered in the negative. So far, no one had been scratched, though the same thing could not be said of their attackers, many of whom were now strewn in the water and on the ground before them.

"How are you doing on bullets?" Pearlie asked. "Do all of you have enough?"

"I'm running out of ammunition," Barrett said.

Pearlie took off his belt and started pushing cartridges out of the little leather loops. "Let's divide up what we have left," he suggested.

"Looks like they're about to come at us again," Billy called out.

"All right, boys, get ready. They're comin' back," Pearlie shouted.

Pearlie got down behind the fallen tree and rested the barrel of his rifle on the log. He thumbed back the hammer of his rifle, sighted down the long barrel, and waited.

The outlaws came again, their horses leaping over the bodies of their comrades and horses who had fallen before. One of the bandits was wearing a blue Army jacket with sergeant's stripes on each sleeve. That was the one Pearlie selected as his target. He waited for a good shot.

When the shot he was looking for presented itself, Pearlie squeezed the trigger. His bullet hit the man just above the right ear, then exited through the top of his head. Pearlie saw brain tissue, blood, and bone detritus erupt from the top of the man's head. The bandit dropped his pistol as he pitched back off his horse.

When they saw their leader go down, the others milled about for a moment, uncertain as to what they should do. One or two started forward, but it wasn't a concerted charge and, like their leader, they were easily shot down.

By now, nearly a dozen outlaws lay dead on both banks of the creek, in the water, and on the sandy beaches of the island. So far, not one of Pearlie's men had been lost, but they were running critically low on ammunition.

Across the water, Pearlie saw that another man was rallying the bandits. At first, Pearlie didn't have a very good view of him. Then the man turned, and Pearlie recognized him.

It was Waco Jones, the same man who had challenged him at the dance back in Corpus Christi.

It was beginning to look as if Waco would get the bandits organized for another charge. If he did, that would be bad, because the defenders didn't have enough ammunition to hold them off. That was when Pearlie got an idea.

"Hey!" Pearlie shouted. "Waco, let's talk!"

Startled to hear himself called by his name, Waco turned toward the island.

"Talk about what? Who are you?"

"I'm the man you challenged to a gunfight back at the dance in Corpus Christi, remember?"

"No, I don't remember," Waco said. "There's never been anyone I challenged who lived to tell the tale."

"I didn't have a gun then," Pearlie called back. "So I wouldn't fight you. But I've got one now."

"Do you? Well, that's good, because you're going to need it," Waco said.

"How 'bout you 'n me havin' that gunfight now?" Pearlie suggested. Then, thinking about Sally and her insistence on proper grammar, he reworded his question. "How about you and *I* having that gunfight now?" he said.

"Hell, seems to me like we *are* havin' us a gunfight," Waco said.

"No, we're having a battle," Pearlie said. "You might get killed on your next charge, and I might not be the one who did it. I don't like that idea. I want to know that I am the one who killed you."

"How do you propose to do that?"

"Let's meet in the middle of the stream," Pearlie suggested. "We'll draw against each other, just the way you wanted."

"Huh-uh," Waco replied.

"What's the matter, Waco? Are you afraid?" Pearlie laughed. "I figured as much. I've got a pretty good nose for who is real and who is bluster. And you, my friend, are all bluster. Or else, you are a coward. No wonder you challenged me when I didn't have a gun. I hear you are some kind of a gunfighter. How many unarmed men have you gunned down? You are a coward, Waco."

"A coward, huh? All right, mister, if you want the others to watch you get shot down. Meet me in the middle of the stream."

"Waco, no," one of the other outlaws said. "Can't you see he's just baitin' you?"

"Yeah?" Waco replied. "Well, you ever seen bait that didn't get eaten? You just sit back and enjoy the show."

"One thing, Waco," Pearlie said.

"What's that?"

"Tell the others that if I beat you, they are to let us ride out of here."

"You heard 'im, boys," Waco said. "If he kills me, let the others ride out." He paused for a moment, then added with a chuckle, "After you kill him, that is."

"Pearlie, no, that's not good odds," Barrett said. "You do it his way, you die, no matter what."

Pearlie checked the loads in his cylinders. He had only two bullets left.

"But they might let you go," Pearlie said.

"No," Barrett said. "It isn't worth it. Don't do it."

"I don't have any choice," Pearlie said as he stood up with his hands in the air. "All right, Waco," he called. "I'm coming out now."

Pearlie walked to the middle of the stream, then stopped. Waco walked toward him, stopping when he was about twenty yards away.

Pearlie thought of the two remaining bear claws he had in his saddlebag. He wished now that he had eaten them.

In the distance, he heard a crow call.

Downstream, a fish splashed in the water.

"Well, you just goin' to stand there all day?" Waco asked.

"I'm waiting on you," Pearlie replied.

"Huh-uh. It's your move, cowboy," Waco said, a mirthless smile on his face.

Pearlie started for his gun. He was fast, but Waco was faster, and even as Pearlie was squeezing the trigger of his own pistol, he saw the puff of smoke, and felt the heavy impact of the bullet as it punched into his chest. He felt the breath leave his body as he pitched backward. He could hear the echo of the two shots reverberating back from the trees and hills.

Then he heard, and felt, nothing.

Barrett and the others looked on in stunned silence as they watched Pearlie fall back into the water. A little puddle of red swirled around him as the water passed over the wound in his chest. Barrett looked at Waco, hoping to see that he too was grievously wounded, but saw only a red mark on his cheek where the bullet had come close enough to burn his skin, but not close enough to wound him.

Waco put the back of his hand to his cheek, then brought it down to examine the blood.

"Damn. The son of a bitch came a lot closer than I thought he would," Waco said. Looking up, he saw Barrett staring in shock at Pearlie's prostrate form.

"Pearlie?" Barrett called. He got no answer.

"You people on the island, is there anyone left who can talk for you?"

"What do you want?" Barrett asked.

"I want you to go back to the ranch. Tell Smoke Jensen what just happened here. Tell him if he wants to revenge his friend, I'll be happy to give him the opportunity."

"You're . . . you're going to let us go?" Barrett asked.

"Yeah," Waco answered. "You just deliver the message like I said."

Chapter Twenty-three

Sally stood in their bedroom, illuminated only by the pool of silver moonlight that spilled in through the window. She wiped the tears from her eyes.

"He's . . . he's not going to make it, is he?" she asked.

Smoke was lying on the bed, his hands laced behind his head, staring up at the moon patterns projected on the ceiling.

"I don't know," Smoke answered. He sighed. "The doctor doesn't give him much hope."

"He hasn't spoken a word since he was brought home," Sally said. "Oh, Smoke, what if we . . . what if we lose him?"

"We'll go on," Smoke said. "Come to bed and get some sleep. Maybe things will be better in the morning."

"All right," Sally agreed. "It doesn't help him for me to stay up all night worrying about him."

Not until Sally's deep, measured breathing told Smoke that she was sound asleep did he get up. Then, walking quietly down the hall, he tapped lightly on the door to Cal's room.

The door opened immediately.

"Any change?" Cal asked.

Smoke shook his head. "No," he said.

"What is it? What's up?"

"We have work to do," Smoke replied.

Cal dressed quickly, then strapped on his gun and followed Smoke down the stairs, walking quietly so as not to awaken anyone else in the house.

"Where are we going?" Cal asked.

"Out there," Smoke replied, pointing to the machine shed.

Even before they got there, Cal could see that there were nearly a dozen people gathered, working in the dim light of a few candles. King was there, as was Kleberg. So were Ramon, Barrett, and several others.

"What's going on?" Cal asked. "Why is everyone here?"

"I asked them to get some things ready for me," Smoke said.

It wasn't until they went around the corner of the machine shed that Cal saw what was going on. He gasped at the sight before him.

There, in a military line, were two Gatling guns and two artillery pieces, caisson-mounted and hitched to teams. The artillery pieces had, in addition to the gun, the ammunition limber. King looked up with a broad, proud grin.

"I wondered if these things would ever be useful to me," he said, pointing to the guns. "Now it looks as if that question is being answered."

"They're ready to go?" Smoke asked.

"Ready to go," King replied.

Smoke walked over to one of the Napoleon 32-pounders, and ran his hand along the smooth lines of the tapered barrel. He turned back to the gathered men, all of whom were looking at him with eager and expectant expressions on their faces.

"Ramon, what about Concepcion?" Smoke asked.

"All of the villagers have moved out, Señor," Ramon replied.

"You are sure that all the villagers have moved?"

"*Sí*. If any have stayed, then they are *colaboradores,* with the enemy."

"You have no problems with what I have in mind?"

"No, Señor. For Emilio I do this. For Pearlie I do this. For all my friends who have been killed by these *hombres malvados* I do this."

"All right, let's saddle up and get mounted," Smoke said. "If we ride hard we will get there by dawn."

Brad Preston stepped out of the toilet, still buttoning his trousers. He had a headache from too much drinking the night before. He knew he shouldn't drink so much, but there was little else to do now, since all the women had left. Even the whores had left Concepcion.

Preston had been having second thoughts about being here. Brandt had promised them all a lot of money, but so far, the only thing that happened was that several of the men who had agreed to ride with Brandt had been killed. Preston's concern over the way things were going led him to have a conversation with Brandt. He tried to talk Brandt into moving things up by having one large raid against Richard King's ranch.

"We could attack in the middle of the night, the way we did before. Only this time, we shouldn't waste our time with the Mexican workers. This time we should go right for the big house itself," Preston suggested.

"That would accomplish nothing,"

Brandt replied. "Don't lose sight of our mission. Our mission is to steal the herd. And the best time to steal the herd is when they start their drive. That's where the money is."

"Yeah," Preston agreed after he thought about it for a few minutes. "Yeah, you're right."

Preston was recalling the conversation that had taken place last night in the Gato Rojo Saloon. He intended to pass it on, word for word, to the men in his company. They too were beginning to get antsy with the long delay in the ultimate payoff.

As he was walking back toward the hotel, he heard a strange sound, rather like the sound a railcar makes when it is rolling, empty, down the track. Puzzled, he looked around to see what it might be.

Out of the corner of his eye, Preston saw something black plunge through the shake roof of the apothecary just across the street from the hotel where he was staying. About one second later, the building exploded in a burst of flame, smoke, and noise. He stood there, glued to his spot, watching, transfixed, as little pieces of the destroyed building came fluttering back down.

Within seconds after that blast, he heard, once more, the rushing noise he had heard

318

earlier. This time the front of the general store went up.

"What in the hell?" Preston asked, running out into the street to see what was going on.

Now he heard the sound of distant thunder, followed, yet again, by the rushing sound. This time, he saw a ball smash into the very hotel where he had been staying. It exploded with a loud roar, followed by screams of pain from several of the men. A second ball, very close behind the first, slammed into the hotel as well. Nearly half the hotel came down and men, who but seconds before had been sleeping, yelled in terror as they spilled out of the collapsed building.

Brandt came running into the street then, strapping on his saber. He watched, in shock, as the hotel came crashing down, killing and wounding several of his men. That was followed almost immediately by another explosion, this one at the far end of the street, and though it wasn't close enough to do him any harm, it did send shards of shrapnel whistling by.

"Artillery!" Brandt shouted. "Who the hell is shooting at us with artillery?"

Two more shells came screaming into the little village, and two more buildings went up. By now, nearly half a dozen of the buildings were burning.

Brandt ran back into the saloon where he had set up his own quarters, then, a moment later, reappeared carrying a telescope.

"Major, what is happening? What should we do?" Pettis asked.

"Get the men together and wait for my orders!" Brandt yelled back over his shoulder as he ran toward the church.

Brandt climbed the ladder into the bell tower, then, from that elevated position, looked to the north of town in the direction from which the shelling was coming.

"Two guns," he said aloud as he saw the two artillery pieces. "I thought so."

The pattern of the shelling, the way two rounds would come in . . . a pause . . . then two more rounds, had made him think that there were only two guns involved. Now he verified that by actual observation.

As he looked at the guns he saw too that there were very few people involved. Each gun had a crew of three men, and there was one man who seemed to be in charge.

"Seven men?" he said. "That fool dares to attack me with only seven men?"

Quickly, Brandt climbed back down, then ran out into the street.

"Corporal Jones!" he called to Waco.

"Yes, sir?"

"Get the men saddled."

"We ain't runnin', are we, Major?" Pettis asked.

"Hell, no, we aren't running," Brandt replied. "We're going to attack."

"Attack? Attack cannons?" Preston asked.

"Yes," Brandt said. "There are only seven men out there. The fools don't realize it, but they have just delivered two guns to us."

Three thousand yards north of town, Smoke watched the two gun crews as they loaded and fired their guns. They worked with the well-oiled efficiency of men who had been drilled in the operation of the pieces, and indeed they had been. In the town Smoke could see smoke coming from nearly a dozen buildings now. He didn't know how many of the outlaws, if any, he had killed with the artillery bombardment, but he intended to keep up the firing as long as his ammunition held out.

Then, as he was watching, he saw what he had hoped to see. Brandt was coming out of the city with all his men.

"Well, Major Brandt, you . . . military genius . . . you. You have made your first big mistake, and I have you," Smoke said with a satisfied smile.

Smoke watched as Brandt paused just outside the city to form his men into a parade-front formation. He was going to launch a cavalry charge against the two guns.

"Smoke?" Barrett said.

"Yes, I see them," Smoke said. "Load the guns with canister."

This time the rounds that were put down the barrel of the two guns were cylindrical, rather than ball-shaped. The cylinders, Smoke knew, were like two giant shotgun shells. They were filled, not with small shot, but with scores of bullet-sized projectiles.

Suddenly, from the other side of the open field, he heard the faint call of "Charge!"

Brandt's entire army came galloping across the field in parade-front formation. The horses' hooves made a thunder across the field, and Smoke watched as the riders, small in the distance, began growing larger and larger as they approached. By now they were close enough that Smoke could see the individual faces of the riders.

"Cal! Ramon!" Smoke shouted.

"Here, Smoke!" Cal answered from a clump of trees to his right.

"Ready, Señor Jensen!" Ramon called from a cluster of bushes to his left.

"Run your guns out and be ready to fire at my command," Smoke ordered.

From his left and his right, the two Gatling guns, which had been concealed by low-lying mesquite trees, were run out, then at the approaching army.

Smoke waited until they had closed to within less than one hundred yards.

"Now! Fire!" he shouted, shooting his own pistol, even as he gave the command. He saw Brandt suddenly get a shocked expression on his face as he realized he had been hit, and hit mortally.

Even as the two cannons roared, and the Gatling guns opened up, Brandt was tumbling from his saddle.

The effect of the four guns on the attacking army was devastating. Nearly one dozen men tumbled from their saddles at the opening volley.

The cannons had to reload, but the Gatling guns continued to rattle away at what was left of Brandt's men. Some of Brandt's men attempted to return fire; others attempted to evacuate the field, but were shot down trying to do so. Smoke was sure that he saw at least three make it back into town and relative safety.

"Cease fire! Cease fire!" Smoke shouted, holding his hands out toward the two Gatling guns, which, by now, were the only two weapons that were still firing.

The guns stopped firing then, and an eerie silence fell across the field. With his gun in his hand, Smoke began walking through the dead, looking down at the bodies. Some of the bodies were so badly mutilated — having been hit several times by the heavy shot — that even if Smoke had known them, he wouldn't have recognized them.

A few were groaning, including the one who was wearing an Army officer's uniform.

"You would be Brandt?" Smoke asked, staring down at him.

"I am," Brandt said. He was holding his hands over his stomach, and as he pulled them away, the palms of his hands formed cups of blood that spilled down the front of his jacket. "My jacket," he grunted.

"Yeah, it is sort of messed up, isn't it?" Smoke said.

"Please, clean it, before you bury me in it."

Smoke snorted a mirthless laugh. "You want me to dishonor the United States Army by burying you in uniform? Not a chance. You'll be lucky if you get buried at all."

If Brandt heard Smoke's comment, he gave no indication of it. He couldn't give an indication of anything, because he was dead.

Preston and Pettis were also dead, as were over thirty other men. They lay scattered all over the ground that had become the impromptu battlefield. Behind the dead, the little village of Concepcion — the earlier fires having been unchecked — was now totally invested. There was not one building that remained undamaged.

Cal came over to stand beside Smoke.

"What do we do now, Smoke?"

"Captain King won't have any trouble getting his herd to market now," Smoke answered. "Our job is finished here. It's time we take Pearlie home."

"What if . . . uh . . . what if Pearlie is dead?" Cal asked.

"We're taking him home," Smoke answered. "Dead or alive, we are taking him home."

Cal nodded his approval. "Yes," he said. "If it was me lying back there, I would want you to take me home as well."

Because of its soft spring ride, Captain King made his carriage available to Smoke so Pearlie would not be jostled about on the trip to the railroad depot in Corpus Christi.

Pearlie was still alive, and had shown a few moments of consciousness during the long, slow ride into town. But now, as they waited on the depot platform for the train, he was as uncommunicative as he had been at any time since he was shot.

"I know exactly where I want to bury him," Sally said. "Out by . . ."

"That stand of aspens, the ones that turn gold in the fall," Smoke said, completing her sentence.

"Yes. It is so beautiful there," Sally said.

"He'll like it there," Cal said as he wiped away a tear. "I've seen him standin' right there on that very spot many times."

"I wonder if he's still . . ." Sally started, but she couldn't finish.

"I'll go check on him," Cal said.

"I think I'll step into the depot to get a cup of coffee," Smoke said. "Would you like a cup?"

"No, thank you," Sally answered.

Smoke was just coming out of the depot carrying a cup of coffee in his right hand when he heard someone call out to him.

"Turn around, Smoke Jensen. I don't want it being said that Waco Jones shot you in the back."

Smoke turned toward his challenger and saw Waco standing just off the edge of the loading dock. Waco wasn't holding a gun, but he did have his hand and fingers curled over the handle of his pistol.

Waco chuckled.

"You seem to be havin' yourself a little problem, don't you?" Waco said.

"What do you mean?" Smoke asked easily, taking a sip of his coffee.

Waco was used to seeing fear in the faces of those that he challenged. He did not see the slightest flicker of fear in Smoke's expression. On the contrary, Smoke was standing there as calmly as if they were discussing the weather.

"What I mean is, you are standin' there holding onto that coffee cup, when you should be holdin' onto a pistol."

"Oh," Smoke replied, holding the cup out. "Don't worry about that. If I need my pistol, I can get to it soon enough."

"Why don't we just see?" Waco said.

Waco's hand dipped toward his pistol grip. It didn't have far to go; he already had it open just above the pistol handle. He felt the satisfaction of wrapping his fingers around the pistol grip, then felt the smooth, well-oiled extraction of the pistol from its holster. He was thumbing back the hammer as he raised his pistol.

Suddenly, the easy, confident smile that

had been on Waco's face was gone. It was replaced by an expression of shock and fear.

The cup of coffee was now in Smoke's left hand, and his pistol was in his right! How the hell did he do that?

Waco tried to pull the trigger but he couldn't. Even as his brain was sending the signal to his trigger finger, he felt a blow to his chest, as if he had been kicked by a mule. He slumped forward, with his pistol dangling by its trigger guard from his finger.

He felt another blow to his right knee, and even before he could react to it, he was hit in the left knee. He went down then, and looking up, saw Smoke standing over him, pointing a smoking gun at his head.

Smoke cocked his pistol, and Waco waited for the final blow that would end his life.

Smoke stood there for a long moment, then, with a sigh of disgust, put his pistol back in his holster.

"Finish me off," Waco said. "Please, finish me off. Don't let me lie here like this."

"Nah," Smoke said. "I have a feelin' they're serving supper in hell about now. If I let you hang around here for a little longer, you'll be late for it. And I want you to miss it."

Smoke started back toward the depot,

and had taken no more than three or four steps when he saw Sally raising her rifle and shooting. Spinning around, he saw that Waco had sat up and raised his pistol, intending to shoot Smoke in the back. He was now clutching a bullet wound in his neck. He fell back, with his gun hand flopped out by his side.

Sally's quick action had saved Smoke's life.

By now the crowd, which had scattered when the shooting started, began to reappear.

"Did you see that?" someone asked. "I mean the way he switched that cup of coffee from one hand to the other. Damn, I ain't never seen nothing like that!"

"What you just seen was the two fastest gunmen there is, goin' after one another," one of the others said.

Cal came up then, just as the train whistle announced its arrival.

"Are you all right?" Cal asked.

"Yes, thanks to Sally," Smoke said, reaching out to put his arm around her and pull her closer to him. "How is Pearlie?"

"I don't know," Cal answered. "About the same, I guess."

"Did he react any to the shooting?" Sally asked.

"No, ma'am, he didn't," Cal answered. "Smoke, is Pearlie going to die?"

"I don't know, Cal," Smoke said. "I don't reckon it's in our hands. All we can do now is get him on the train and take him home."

Carefully, very carefully, they loaded Pearlie onto the parlor car, laying him gently on a bed in one of the bedrooms. Then, with all passengers loaded, the engineer gave two short blasts on the whistle and the train pulled out of the station.

Smoke settled in his seat and looked out at the rather barren West Texas land they were passing through. It would be good to get home.

Afterword

Notes from the Old West

In the small town where I grew up, there were two movie theaters. The Pavilion was one of those old-timey movie palaces, built in the heyday of Mary Pickford and Charlie Chaplin — the silent era of the 1920s. By the 1950s, when I was a kid, the Pavilion was a little worn around the edges, but it was still the premier theater in town. They played all those big Technicolor biblical Cecil B. DeMille epics and corny MGM musicals. In Cinemascope, of course.

On the other side of town was the Gem, a somewhat shabby and run-down grind house with sticky floors and torn seats. Admission was a quarter. The Gem booked low-budget "B" pictures (remember the Bowery Boys?), war movies, horror flicks, and Westerns. I liked the Westerns best. I could usually be found every Saturday at the Gem, along with my best friend, Newton

Trout, watching Westerns from 10 a.m. until my father came looking for me around suppertime. (Sometimes Newton's dad was dispatched to come fetch us.) One time, my dad came to get me right in the middle of *Abilene Trail*, which featured the now-forgotten Whip Wilson. My father became so engrossed in the action, he sat down and watched the rest of it with us. We didn't get home until after dark, and my mother's meat loaf was a pan of gray ashes by the time we did. Though my father and I were both in the doghouse the next day, this remains one of my fondest childhood memories. There was Wild Bill Elliot, Gene Autry, and Roy Rogers, and Tim Holt, and, a little later, Rod Cameron and Audie Murphy. Of these newcomers, I never missed an Audie Murphy Western, because Audie was sort of an antihero. Sure, he stood for law and order and was an honest man, but sometimes he had to go around the law to uphold it. If he didn't play fair, it was only because he felt hamstrung by the laws of the land. Whatever it took to get the bad guys, Audie did it. There were no finer points of law, no splitting of legal hairs. It was instant justice, devoid of long-winded lawyers, bored or biased jurors, or black-robed, often corrupt judges.

Steal a man's horse and you were the guest of honor at a necktie party.

Molest a good woman and you got a bullet in the heart or a rope around the gullet. Or at the very least, you got the crap beat out of you. Rob a bank and you faced a hail of bullets or the hangman's noose.

Saved a lot of time and money, did frontier justice.

That's all gone now, I'm sad to say. Now you hear, "Oh, but he had a bad childhood" or, "His mother didn't give him enough love" or, "The homecoming queen wouldn't give him a second look and he has an inferiority complex." Or, "cultural rage," as the politically correct bright boys refer to it. How many times have you heard some self-important defense attorney moan, "The poor kids were only venting their hostilities toward an uncaring society?"

Mule fritters, I say. Nowadays, you can't even call a punk a punk anymore. But don't get me started.

It was "Howdy, ma'am" time, too. The good guys, antihero or not, were always respectful to the ladies. They might shoot a bad guy five seconds after tipping their hat to a woman, but the code of the West demanded you be respectful to a lady.

Lots of things have changed since the

heyday of the Wild West, haven't they? Some for the good, some for the bad.

I didn't have any idea at the time that I would someday write about the Old West. I just knew that I was captivated by the Old West.

When I first got the itch to write, back in the early 1970s, I didn't write Westerns. I started by writing horror and action adventure novels. After more than two dozen novels, I began thinking about developing a Western character. From those initial musings came the novel *The Last Mountain Man: Smoke Jensen*. That was followed by *Preacher: The First Mountain Man*. A few years later, I began developing the Last Gunfighter series. Frank Morgan is a legend in his own time, the fastest gun west of the Mississippi . . . a title and a reputation he never wanted, but can't get rid of.

The Gunfighter series is set in the waning days of the Wild West. Frank Morgan is out of time and place, but still, he is pursued by men who want to earn a reputation as the man who killed the legendary gunfighter. All Frank wants to do is live in peace. But he knows in his heart that dream will always be just that: a dream, fog and smoke and mirrors, something elusive that will never really come to fruition. He will be forced to wander the West, alone, until one day his luck runs out.

For me, and for thousands — probably millions — of other people (although many will never publicly admit it), the old Wild West will always be a magic, mysterious place: a place we love to visit through the pages of books; characters we would like to know . . . from a safe distance; events we would love to take part in — again, from a safe distance. For the old West was not a place for the faint of heart. It was a hard, tough, physically demanding time. There were no police to call if one faced adversity. One faced trouble alone, and handled it alone. It was rugged individualism: something that appeals to many of us.

I am certain that is something that appeals to most readers of Westerns.

I still do on-site research (whenever possible) before starting a Western novel. I have wandered over much of the West, prowling what is left of ghost towns. Stand in the midst of ruins of these old towns, use a little bit of imagination, and one can conjure up life as it used to be in the Wild West. The rowdy Saturday nights, the tinkling of a piano in a saloon, the laughter of cowboys and miners letting off steam after a week of hard work. Use a little more imagination and one can envision two men standing in the street, facing one another, seconds before the hook and draw of a gunfight. A moment later, one is dead and the other rides away.

The old, wild, untamed West.

There are still some ghost towns to visit, but they are rapidly vanishing as time and the elements take their toll. If you want to see them, make plans to do so as soon as possible, for in a few years, they will all be gone.

And so will we.

Stand in what is left of the Big Thicket country of eastern Texas and try to imagine how in the world the pioneers managed to get through that wild tangle. I have wondered that many times and marveled at the courage of the men and women who slowly pushed westward, facing dangers that we can only imagine.

Let me touch briefly on a subject that is very close to me: firearms. There are some so-called historians who are now claiming that firearms played only a very insignificant part in the settlers' lives. They claim that only a few were armed. What utter, stupid nonsense! What do these so-called historians think the pioneers did for food? Do they think the early settlers rode down to the nearest supermarket and bought their meat? Or maybe they think the settlers chased down deer or buffalo on foot and beat the animals to death with a club. I have a news flash for you so-called historians: The settlers used guns to shoot their game. They used guns to defend hearth and home against Indians on the warpath. They used guns to protect themselves from outlaws. Guns are a part of Americana. And always will be.

The mountains of the West and the remains of the ghost towns that dot those areas are some of my favorite subjects to write about. I have done extensive research on the various mountain ranges of the West and go back whenever time permits. I sometimes stand surrounded by the towering mountains and wonder how in the world the pioneers ever made it through. As hard as I try and as often as I try, I simply cannot imagine the hardships those men and women endured over the hard months of their incredible journey. None of us can. It is said that on the Oregon Trail alone, there are at least two bodies in lonely, unmarked graves for every mile of that journey. Some students of the West say the number of dead is at least twice that. And nobody knows the exact number of wagons that impatiently started out alone and simply vanished on the way, along with their occupants, never to be seen or heard from again.

Just vanished.

The one-hundred-and-fifty-year-old ruts of the wagon wheels can still be seen in various places along the Oregon Trail. But if you plan to visit those places, do so quickly, for they are slowly disappearing. And when they are gone, they will be lost forever, except in the words of Western writers.

As long as I can peck away at a keyboard and find a company to publish my work, I will not let the Old West die. That I promise you.

The West will live on as long as there are writers willing to write about it, and publishers willing to publish it. Writing about the West is wide open, just like the old Wild West. Characters abound, as plentiful as the wide-open spaces, as colorful as a sunset on the Painted Desert, as restless as the eversighing winds. All one has to do is use a bit of imagination. Take a stroll through the cemetery at Tombstone, Arizona; read the inscriptions. Then walk the main street of that once-infamous town around midnight and you might catch a glimpse of the ghosts that still wander the town. They really do. Just ask anyone who lives there. But don't be afraid of the apparitions; they won't hurt you. They're just out for a quiet stroll.

The West lives on. And as long as I am alive, it always will.

William Johnstone

About the Author

William W. Johnstone is the *USA Today* bestselling author of over 130 books, including the popular *Ashes*, *Mountain Man*, and *Last Gunfighter* series.